EAGLEMAN

Baba Hassan

First published in 2022 by 'Cyrus Sage Publishing'.

ISBN: 979-88212129-55

Table of Contents

Chapter 1

Across The Skies, an eagle's shadow flutters across the silhouette of a statue on the sign. It lands on its shoulders.

Cyrus (Narration):

"Allow him to stay for his angelic judgment view on the afterlife and although it has not met its death and passed the paths, the dark evil starless spirits disappear and that is when we reunite in paradise, as The Eagle foretells."

The Eagle lands on the shoulder of a figure perched atop a rundown two-story tenement building.

A sound of a rumbling engine and booming opera precedes the arrival of an ominous black hot rod hearse down a building of a dead-end street in Eagle City. It is night-time, Maverick who has a small hunchback, is in a black chauffeur's uniform. He opens the driver's side door and steps around to the passenger's side rear door and opens it. A tall sixty-year-old Wizard Priest called, Big Daddy Jesse Sparrow steps out from the car. Appearing in his black hair and razor-sharp features, Big Daddy is accented by long jagged sideburns and a pointed goatee. Maverick stares at him and looks at him as he fixes his priest's suit and collar. Big Daddy looks at him weirdly, "What are you looking at? Come on. You got the backpack. Right?"

Maverick answers, "Yes, Sir. It's safe with me."

"Alright. Come with me." Maverick walks behind Big Daddy up the steps and into the building. The halls are lined with flickering candles on both sides. Maverick limps after Big Daddy up the creaky stairs to the second floor. They get to the flat hallway as Maverick gasps, "God Almighty! People who live here must love the area. Huh?"

"You just listen to me! If I want your stupid point of view, I'll ask but for now, just do what I pay you to and shut up!" Big Daddy responds harshly.

Maverick hunches in humility, "Yes, Sir. I do apologize." Big Daddy stops before a door adorned with strange voodoo paraphernalia. They hear loud noises of sex coming from the room. Big Daddy pounds on the door with his fist and waits for a response. Shortly, a Bald Man opens the door, sticking his head out. Big Daddy pushes him aside and barges his way in. Maverick follows him inside. Big Daddy and Maverick look around and see festive decorations, piles of junk, old newspapers and garbage. They look at the birdcages and see that there are stuffed with chickens hanging from the ceiling and overfed cats lying everywhere. Meanwhile, an ill-tempered dwarf called, Ethan sits on the sofa. He is watching four different television screens playing different porn films. An armless old man is sitting next to him breathing from his oxygen tank standing at the edge of the couch. Ethan acknowledges Big Daddy with a slight nod and goes back to watching the television. Maverick follows Big Daddy down a long hallway and notices a taxidermist's dream, lined with every dead animal imaginable. He sees a dead dog crucified on a heavy wooden door at the end of it. His attention is interrupted when Big Daddy snaps his fingers and motions for the backpack to be handed over to him. Maverick obediently hands the backpack over to Big Daddy who addresses him with a slight turn of his head to the side, "Get back to the car. I'll be out after I meet Eve."

Maverick nods and limps back down the hall as Big Daddy approaches and knocks on another room door. He hears a female voice from inside, "Who is it?"

"Big Daddy." He answers impatiently. An old witch, Eve Pearls, opens the door. Big Daddy enters and shuts the door behind him. Inside the room, he stands opposite her over a bizarre cauldron shaped like a three-headed wolf. Swirling smoke and brilliant beams of light pour forth and illuminate strange sculptures of demonic figures in the room. Big Daddy glances at the figures which seem to come to life when they are hit by the powerful light. Big Daddy opens the backpack and removes a bundle wrapped in plastic. Eve looks at him when she notices the movement, "Come on. Pass it over. Pass it over to me."

Big Daddy stretches his hand to hand the package, "It's the final one."

"Yeah. It's the seventh one. Isn't it? It's good to know that number. The ring has presently concluded. Everything should be in place and everything will be ready to move forward," She responds as she takes the package from him.

She unwraps the plastic to reveal a baby which has a second, tiny deformed head growing from its neck. Eve smiles, "Interesting...It is adorable. Isn't it? Especially when you have not one but two heads." Suddenly, Eve drops the baby in the cauldron which causes the room to explode with a fiery light. They stare into the vapours, their eyes turn completely white, as though they are possessed. While in possession, Eve echoes with a loud voice, "I can see the Demon King is proud of you, Big Daddy. I can see his jagged frosted fangs reaching out with wonderful smiles. He has all the solutions you were looking for. Ghostly souls are arriving in the growing vapour as we speak."

Big Daddy replies in a deeper voice, "Come on. Let it out. I need to know what's going on! I've been longing for these solutions for a long time. So, tell me, are my visions genuinely telling me the sign of forthcoming events? Are you saying I am looking at my future imminently?"

"Here's the thing, Big Daddy. If you want to know what's in store for you.... why don't you have a look at it yourself? After all, it is your future." Suddenly, the ghostly souls shoot into Big Daddy's body. He goes into a delusional state which causes his eyes to turn red with blood oozing from them. He sees a death montage of the world's terrifying future. He also sees diseases control workers in plague suits collecting bodies and burning them. A vision of him walking among the horror feeling unaffected as he thrives in it pops in. Next, he sees himself as an old self preaching to a small crowd at an abandoned building with a flowing robe inside a makeshift church. A large crowd is in front of him and mesmerized by the preaching. His future self says, "Amazing....my prophecy.... the wonderful dreams of death upon death.... sorrow upon sorrow.... the earth's soil hurting in the pits below my porch in the final call away. I shall reconstruct my sanctuary on this earth and the portals of the underworld will be unable to conquer it. I, Big Daddy Jesse Sparrow, am incarnate and my spirits have returned. I am breathing air comfortably everlastingly while I hold the passports of the dead souls and the underworld....so my servants will be aware of the sun up of a new day. The pagans accountable for our hardship will be revealed and...."

As Big Daddy preaches, several people are standing next to large wooden gallows ready for an execution by hanging. His hair is long and grey showing the many years he has been living. He continues to address the crowd, ".... killed. On the devil's watch, we will chastise the sinners and purge our universe of devilish slaves." The floor drops open and they fall. Their necks snap collectively like a clap of thunder. The crowd roars and chants Big Daddy's name with their hands raised while Big Daddy overlooks them with pride. Big Daddy continues, "We represent the dominance of revulsion, virginal chastity, angelic fire.... resembling a velour protection chained shape, grabbing the neck of a bad, weak universe.... a universe where the spiritless receive nothing but deathless agony and grievance endlessly."

Suddenly, lightning crashes in Eve's room. Big Daddy comes back to reality from the future. The lights subside as the smoke settles. Big Daddy and Eve's eyes return to normal. Big Daddy tries to blink repeatedly to improve his vision, "Wow....This is amazing. I can't believe this is actually happening."

Eve replies, "Your dream will come true, Big Daddy. What you saw was not plain illusions. What you saw were revelations." Big Daddy asks, "So when....is it happening?"

"It will happen in due time, Big Daddy. It won't be long before the mouth of the underworld breaks its portal and the sheets of destiny shall be on your hands. Big Daddy, you are going to be one of the lucky ones who will deliver a champion arrow."

Suddenly, something new in the vapours catches Eve's attention. Eve squints to have a better look, "Hold on. This can't be true."

"What can't be true? What's going on? What have you seen? There are more to this than meets the eye. Doesn't it?" He asks.

Eve develops a worried look on her face, "I saw a hurdle standing in your way, Big Daddy. It's very vague but I saw.... your enemy." As more smoke belches from the cauldron, a faint image form.

Simultaneously, out on the street, children in fancy dress costumes are running by a house. A friendly figure is propped in the well-kept yard. A five-year-old Indian boy, Cyrus Eagleman, is helping his adoptive white mother, Mrs Eagleman. She is an attractive woman in her mid-forties. He is helping her decorate a birthday cake.

In Eve's Room, Eve stares blankly at the fading smoke, "Your enemy is a little boy. He's very tiny, fragile, vulnerable and weak but despite all of that, he will someday single out the bloodthirsty heirloom that you crave for."

Cyrus continues to decorate the cake and putting candles on it at the top unaware of the activities going on in a flat a few yards away.

Big Daddy gasps in shock as he approaches Eve, "That can't be true, Eve. How is that even possible? How on earth can a kid come between me and my world of supreme dominance...? You can't seriously think that! You can't seriously tell me that this kid is going to ruin my plans?" As Big Daddy and Eve continue to speak, the image grows hazier before them and Eve answers, "I'm afraid I'm unable to clarify that Big Daddy, but you need to trust me on this. There is much more to this kid than meets the eye. There is more to this boy than even I can see. He is a bad omen for you, Big Daddy. He's a hazardous danger!" Upon hearing the revelation, Big Daddy becomes grim and looks on ahead intently while he watches the image of Cyrus's laughable face vanish.

Cyrus is in his house sitting in front of the television. He turns to Mrs Eagleman who is sitting on a couch next to him knitting. He jokes with her, "Hello." She responds, "Yes, Sir. Can I help you?"

"Yes. We got a danger ahead of us," he replies as he fidgets with the remote.

Mrs Eagleman pretends to be amused, "Danger? Really?" Cyrus and Mrs Eagleman break into laughter. They both glance at a framed family portrait of a baby

Cyrus with Mrs Eagleman and his late adoptive white father dressed in a police uniform. They overhear excitement of unknown celebrations coming from children scurrying from house to house outside on the streets.

That evening, Cyrus sits at the kitchen table and eats his food while Mrs Eagleman washes the dishes. Cyrus calls out, "Mom."

Mrs Eagleman replies, "Yeah, Cy?"

"Was it true?"

"What was what true?"

"What Aunt Pam said. Did you and daddy really find me at the orphanage in London and decided to adopt me?"

"No." She sighs as she places a plate on the dish rack.

Cyrus continues to inquire, "Then why am I dark-skinned and you're white?"

She reaches for a towel and dries her hands, "That doesn't matter. You're our son and that is all that matters. Come on. Finish your food." Cyrus shows his band-aid to his mother, "Alright. Can I get this off me?

It makes me look stupid. I don't think The Bogeyman would want to wear a crappy band-aid."

Mrs Eagleman ignores him as she heads to the table, "You know what I think? I think The Bogeyman might not be able to get into a lot of problems at school and you know what?"

Cyrus takes a sip of his juice, "Come on, Mum. You know the reason why I punched that bully is because he was picking on Steve. I had to do something. Daddy used to say we can't let people get away with violence. You won't believe all the horrible and nasty things he said about us."

"I understand what your daddy taught you but not everything he taught you was right. Your daddy wanted you to defend yourself. I wanted you to keep away from trouble and the only you can do that would be taking no notice of them." She puts her hand over his shoulders, "It's not difficult to ignore them. That way, you'll be out of harm's way. Understand?"

Cyrus looks sincere but crosses his fingers behind his back, "Okay but it's not something daddy would agree. Right?" *Now he has made a promise that he is willing to break.*

Mrs Eagleman sighs sadly, "He wouldn't and I understand all of that. Don't think I don't. I only want what's best for you and what's best for you in this respect is being cautious, Cy." She wakes up to inspect his wound, "Come on. I'll need to look at it...." Mrs Eagleman peels the band-aid back, "It looks like it's healed. Alright. Now I need you to swear to me that from this day moving forward, you'll stay away from trouble."

Cyrus turns to her with a smile with his arm on her hand, "Okay. Scout's honour." Mrs Eagleman smiles back, "Alright. Are you all set? On the count of three....one, two...." Before she could get to the three, she rips the band-aid off. Cyrus screams out. "Ow. You fooled me."

Mrs Eagleman winks and tweaks his nose.

As they are sitting in the living room, they hear a knock on the door. Cyrus goes to answer it jumping with excitement as he runs toward the door, "I'm getting it! I'm getting it!" He looks through the peephole as Mrs Eagleman shouts after him, "Confirm who it is through the other side before you open it!"

Cyrus runs down a short hallway to the front door, pulls up a step stool and steps on it. He looks through the peephole. He sees a father and son disguised in fancy dress costumes. The father is dressed as a devil in a red hooded robe along with a grinning mask covering his face while the son is dressed in a creepy-looking clown suit. Cyrus steps off the chair and opens the door. He looks at them as the son stares at him while the father peers inside to see if anyone else is home. Cyrus asks cautiously, "Hi. Can I help you?"

The son stares at Cyrus After a brief comment he inquires, "Hello? If you're after donations, I'm not giving you any until you ask me politely. That's what normal people do when they knock on somebody else's door." The son opens his sack and sings in a deep adult voice, "Can I please have your life in exchange for something precious I can hold on to?"

Suddenly, the son reveals himself to be Ethan and throws his sack over Cyrus's head. He carries Cyrus as he kicks and screams inside the flat. The father removes his mask and it turns out it is Big Daddy. He gets in and shuts the door. Mrs Eagleman screams out in horror as they burst into the television room with Cyrus. Cyrus becomes frightened as he shouts, "Mum!" Mrs Eagleman runs over to Cyrus but stops mid-way when Big Daddy pulls and aims a gun at her.

He commands her, "Don't take one more step because if you do, that'll be the end of your life." Mrs Eagleman stops and becomes mortified, "Alright. Just don't do anything to him. He's just a kid. Leave him alone and take what you need to take from here."

Big Daddy chuckles, "It's funny you said that because that's the reason why I'm here." He signals Ethan, "Get that sack off him. I think it's fair to let the enemy witness their final moments."

Ethan removes the bag from Cyrus's head. His face is revealed smeared with sweat and tears running down his face. Cyrus gets in a state of shock as he numbly blinks uncontrollable at the television. Big Daddy looks at him with grimace, "Well....it seems like I have met my nemesis." Mrs Eagleman gets on her knees to beg for mercy as she sobs away, "No! Please don't do anything to him. He is all I got. Please. Oh, God. Please have mercy on my son. I'll do anything for you...I will do anything you want me to do...."

Big Daddy suddenly turns to her in anger, "Hey! Settle down, Bitch! There isn't anything that you or your almighty up above the skies can do to help you. It's nothing personal. It's just basic procedure. That's all. Now, why don't you just be a nice lonely tramp and have a good nap? It's getting a little late." He turns back to a teary Cyrus, "Bid farewell to your beautiful mum.... because this is the last time you're gonna see her...." Ethan grins and raises his hand, "Sleep tight, mummy."

Without any remorse or hesitation, Big Daddy instantly shoots her on the left side of her chest. The impact causes her to jerk backwards, her head leaning backwards and her chest forward. She falls to her death as a pool of blood gushes from her chest and fills the floor. Cyrus screams out in agony, "Mum! No!"

The room scene is left bizarre with blood spatters on the television screen. Cyrus gets numb with shock while he stares at the screen. Cyrus freaks out and breaks free from Ethan and crawls to Mrs Eagleman's side. He curls up with Mrs Eagleman's body as the television flickers behind them. Big Daddy smirks, "I got to admit....it was really soothing. Wasn't it? It really touched my heart lightly."

Ethan replies with sarcasm, "I couldn't agree more with you, Sir...It was pretty vague, to be honest with you." Big Daddy cocks his gun and steps up toward Cyrus, "Hope you have thought about your final words, Boy." Cyrus stares at Big Daddy hatefully as Big Daddy continues, "No? Oh, well. Very well, Cyrus...I do believe the accursed stupid box has blessed you with the best appropriate eulogy." While Cyrus continues to look up at Big Daddy despicably, Big Daddy lowers his gun straight at Cyrus and he smiles, "Welcome to a modern universe of Angels and Devils." Big Daddy fires his gun at his head. Cyrus falls to the ground and dies instantly. His eyes are left open as Big Daddy and Ethan walk towards the door with zero regrets.

Cyrus (Narration):

"From an everlastingly decade which shadowed, the skies became stygian and glacial. At the same

time, evil and starvation attacked, desolated and destroyed everywhere. The combined powers of fiendishness and insidiousness had developed and risen, transforming the universe into ungodly dark earth of damnation."

Chapter 2

At Cyrus's headstone, The Eagle arrives and lands on it. Cyrus's grave opens and flowers tumble away. The soil on top sinks halfway into the grave. Earthquake like movements tremble as the headstone breaks into two. Suddenly, Cyrus comes back to life and climbs up the grave. His hands emerge out first and the rest of his body crawls out. He claws his hands on the mud while he howls in anguish. As the world takes shape, Cyrus rises from the ground. He suddenly collapses while he writhes and twitches in the mud.

He gets up and looks around but no one seems to be around. The wind blows a few leaves towards him and he looks away, he sees the exit door on the other side. The Eagle flies towards the exit and he follows it. His whole body is covered with mud and his clothes are tattered. He walks away and gets to an alleyway where he climbs up the ladder and slips. Cyrus stumbles across the roof while The Eagle leads him to the stairs along the landing of Cyrus's old house. Cyrus pushes the door open and enters. After getting in, he looks around and finds new photographs of new owners who are currently living there. As Cyrus looks around, memories of his death start to come back which cause him to relive his and Mrs Eagleman's deaths through remembrance. Cyrus experiences those memories agonizingly when he remembers Big Daddy and Ethan barging into the house and throwing a sack over his head. He remembers Big Daddy's antagonizing words before shooting his mother on the chest splattering her guts on the television set. He remembers the smirk on Big Daddy's face after murdering his mother. His heart gets overwhelmed with a painful sensation. As Cyrus continues to get painful memories, he remembers Big Daddy lowering his gun straight at him and shooting him dead before saying, "*Welcome to a modern universe of Angels and Devils.*"

After remembering those painful events, Cyrus looks back at the painful moments that he had with Mrs Eagleman. Visions of the eerie night flash in his mind as the loud gunshot sounds echo in his mind. Suddenly, a middle-aged man, appears at the doorway. He meets a sad looking 10-year-old boy staring at the floor. Harris looks at Cyrus concernedly while Cyrus has his back turned. He slowly approaches Cyrus, "Hello? Who are you?" Cyrus slowly turns his head to Harris who goes ahead and asks, "What are you doing in my house?" Cyrus cries but Harris kneels and puts his jacket over him with remorse, "Hey. Come on. Let's get you cleaned up. Alright?" Harris helps Cyrus up and leads him to the bathroom, "Don't worry. It's only me living in here now. Have a shower. I'll get you something to eat." He leaves Cyrus alone while Cyrus shuts the bathroom door behind him.

THIRTY YEARS LATER

After thirty years, Big Daddy achieved his evil powers through Eve. Eagle City was always governed separately by Michael Colane, The Chief of State. As Big Daddy sought to gain the power he desired throughout the years, he murdered millions of people who do not support his cause and the remaining few live in fear, pain and agony as terror and fury encompass the whole land. Eve Pearls, an Old Witch helped him to summon the evil powers, turning him into the most powerful man in the world. People are no longer allowed to practise their religious beliefs. Instead, they pay their earnings to Big Daddy and whoever tries to defy him is met with death. While people are languishing in poverty, diseases and hunger without the help of the newly-formed selfish government, Big Daddy seeks to get rid of the government in order to gain world dominance. Together with Big Daddy's evil powers and his world influence, Big Daddy has his army of human protectors that guard him 24/7 in return for food and keeping their heads on their necks. Despite this, there are a few groups that try to rebel against him and his evil regime but they cannot fight the supernatural power.

At a Tangle Wood Border, heavy rain falls on a dense black forest throughout the night followed by thick fog that hovers over the ground where scattered tombstones and monuments stick through. The Eagle gallops and takes flight as it swoops across the sky. A dark ghostly figure on a jet-black horse materializes out of the fog. It reveals to be Cyrus who is now a grown man cloaked in black with a cap while The Eagle gets to him and sits on his shoulder.

Cyrus (Narration):

"This is a little odd. Maybe unusual or abnormal is the word. There are certain memories that people look back on and there are certain memories that people decide not to remember. Sometimes, it's easier getting it out of our brains. When I look back at what happened to me, it seems like it only happened last night. It's weird especially when I was working on getting through the dirt and soil.... the ghastly dark shadows encircling me in the nightfall.... the chilled emotionless storm of breeze during the hour of darkness engulfing me as I

snap and split through the depthless and resurface. It seems that all entities are old habitual intelligent life forms that are overshadowed and soared. It also seems like while I was shutting my eyes, someone snatched the entire universe away from God's hands. There are certain moments when broken and crushed memories flashed through my brain and severed from the existing world. I am not certain of what has happened but these memories are either erased from my mind or just mere illusions. It seems like I am a spirited souled shadow lingering in my own nightmares or a deceased apparition that seeks my own self."

At a Cemetery, another shadow rider emerges from the mist behind Cyrus. Cyrus turns to see Harris who is dressed in worn brown leathers and a hooded black poncho. His entire body is covered by a black skeleton tattoo including a black skull on his face. Cyrus and Harris pull their horses off the trail, dismount and tie them to a large cross-shaped headstone. Cyrus moves his head from side to side just over the fog, "He's not far. I can sense the deep reverberating coming through my body."

Harris looks around, "And which direction are we going?" Cyrus points to a horizon over a rise and quickly moves towards the direction. Harris follows him and trips over a headstone. He screams out in pain, "Stupid mist...." Cyrus walks well ahead of Harris as he moves deftly through the graveyard to a broken-down mausoleum. He sees the silhouette of a man who is seemingly ducking behind a headstone over the next rise. As his view gets clearer, Cyrus sees the man pulling his gun out and clicking it. Harris catches up to the man as he huffs and puffs. Harris is about to say something but Cyrus puts a finger on his lips and points to the man's shadow.

Harris draws his gun as he and Cyrus separate and circle up and around both sides of this man. Cyrus and Harris move like shadows among the graves. Instantly, Cyrus slips up behind the man and puts a gun to his head, "Freeze, Stalker." The graveyard is silent and only their beating hearts can be heard as they both breath in and out intensely. The cold barrel of the gun can be felt on this man's back. He knows he has nowhere to hide nor run but he knows that he cannot be taken alive by Cyrus. He slowly turns towards Cyrus with his hands behind his head to show his surrender.

Suddenly, he draws a gun from his back pocket like a flash of lightning and put the barrel into his mouth. The man puts a bullet through his mouth and out through his head. A shocked Cyrus sees blood and brain matter spattered all over the gravestone. Harris arrives in the spur of the moment, "You had him. Didn't you?"

Cyrus nods and then prods the man's head with the barrel of his gun. It slumps to the side to reveal to Harris that he is dead with his eyes gouged out. As Harris looks on, his mouth is frozen open in a scream, "Crikey! Who the hell would do something like this?" They hear a sound from a distance. Harris says, "What do you reckon, Cy? Grave Robbers?"

Cyrus answers, "Don't ask me. How the hell would I know? Your guess is as good as mine. It seemed like he was just roaming around someplace he shouldn't be especially at this time the night." Harris comments, "Maybe he was depressed." Cyrus gestures past Harris as something else catches his attention, "Or it could be that he may be able to give us some answers to the solution that we're looking for."

He points to another body behind Harris with its face down in the dirt and partially obscured by a large headstone. Cyrus and Harris see empty booze bottles strewn around him and clothes soaked with blood. Harris goes over and lifts the dead man's head by the hair. He finds that his eyes are also gone and there is a row of bats tattooed around his neck. Harris gags to the side then says, "Crikey! It's Tom Lemons. Too bad. He did not deserve to go out like this." Harris happily starts to search through his pockets for money. Cyrus continues to examine the corpse, "What? You mean to tell me that you both actually knew each other?"

Harris responds, "Of course we do. Tom and I were trained gunmen during our time in the army. He was a sharpshooter. That was what he specialized in." Cyrus scans the graveyard warily as the wind howls between the headstones and skeletal tree limbs. He looks back at Harris, "I can see a lot of new organic food in this cemetery. We have to knock on your friend's door and end the night before we overstay our visit." Harris continues to check his pockets, "Alright. I will go ahead and free Tom off his assets. I guess he'll not have to worry about them any longer now that he's dead. After that, we'll have a fun time following these tracks."

Cyrus draws his sword and methodically brings it down and as he does, Harris finds a flyer in one of Tom's pockets. His eyes light up while he reads it. Harris whistles pleasantly, "Gotcha!" He hands the flyer to Cyrus who looks at it and sees the title, "MANHUNT: DEAD OR ALIVE - VINNY ALONG WITH EVERY SINGLE DISCIPLES OF THE BLACK TOWERS!" He looks under the title and sees photos of every decrepit member. Harris articulates, "It's unbelievable! That is a lot of money for a cash reward." Cyrus folds the flyer and puts it in his pocket, "Yeah well don't think about spending it just yet. Everyone will be ripping these animals so I think we need to act fast." Harris stashes a few valuables that he picked from Tom, "Okay. Just let me look at the plan chart before we do anything else." Cyrus carries Tom's head by the hair and puts it in an old leather sack strapped over his horse's back. He ties it up and mounts it afterwards, "If I can recall correctly, Vinny was the one who drew the vice."

Harris enters the mausoleum alone and unrolls his plan chart on top of an exposed coffin. He lights a match to illuminate it as he points to a section on the map, "Right. This is where we are. That means Abyss Street goes up to here....and that means the vice should be round about...."

Meanwhile, Cyrus waits on his horse and pulls a cigar out. He bites the end off and spits it out. He strikes a match with his thumbnail and lights it using his cap to block the rain. The match illuminates his painted face and shows his ghostly white face and the white streak in his black hair. A moment later, unbeknownst to him, Cyrus does not notice the three figures slowly approaching from behind as he shouts above the rain, "Hey, Harris! What's the score?! What are you doing up there?! Are you actually reading the plan chart? It seems like you're messing about over there!"

Harris shouts back, "Shut up! Just let me have some time to myself. Will you? I need it especially when I hang out with you all the time." As Cyrus and Harris continue to speak to each other from a distance, sludge from the leaky tomb drips onto the plan chart. Harris brushes it off in annoyance.

Cyrus complains from outside as he lets out a cloud of smoke through his nostrils, "Well whatever you're doing, finish it off now. Vinny along with his cronies aren't going to wait for us you know!"

Harris tries to concentrate but the bickering gets to the best of him, "Come on now! Give me a break! Will you?! In case you hadn't noticed, I was looking for a way to...." Before Harris could finish his sentence, a new plop of sludge lands right on his match and plunges him into darkness. "Oh God Almighty" he complains.

Still, unbeknownst to Cyrus, The Evil Demons walk ahead inches away. He blows out more smoke as he hears a faint sound, "Sorry. You were saying?"

Harris still in the darkness, strikes another match just as a huge splash of Chad lands on his head which shocks him, "What in the name of God is that...?" He raises the match and looks up to the rafters to discover four more evil demons. As Harris stares at them, he first assumes they are corpses but when the light hits them, their eyes pop open. They let out an unholy screeching hiss. Harris gets startled, "Holy Mary! Oh, God!" After that, he steps back only to bump into another evil demon as it reaches out and throttles him.

At the same time outside, Cyrus gets ambushed by the four evil demons. They pull him down off his horse before he can respond. He lands on his back with the evil demons swarming and trying to tear the flesh from his bones. The evil demons find that they are no match for Cyrus's lightning-quick reflexes. Cyrus throws them off, leaps to his feet and draws his sword in one smooth motion. He slices into the neck of the closest evil demon and kills it. Cyrus then jabs his sword behind him and cuts deep into the cold heart of the second evil demon without turning.

Harris is also fighting for his life when a child-demon hangs from his back. He drives a jagged piece of wood from the smashed coffin through the heart of another evil demon. He reaches behind him and throws the child-demon across the room and impales it on the horns of a gargoyle sculpture.

Cyrus continues to slice and dice everything in his path to the mausoleum in an attempt to assist Harris. He is drenched and covered in blood. Two new evil demons try to enter the mausoleum but Harris quickly charges them head-on and grabs each one by the throat.

Cyrus beheads the last of his pack of evil demons and then hears a mighty roar from the mausoleum. He turns to see Harris explode from the mausoleum with two evil demons gripped by the throat on each of his hands. Suddenly, a pair of arms burst from the ground and grab a hold of his legs from out of nowhere. Cyrus shouts out to Harris, "Harris! You need to make sure their heads are up!" The evil demons kick and scream wildly in Harris's grip. Harris shouts back, "I'm actually doing my best here, Cyrus! Does it look like I'm playing around?!"

Cyrus pulls the two daggers strapped to his forearms and skewers them into the head of the evil demon beneath his feet. Harris cries out, "I don't think I can hang on to these idiots for any longer!"

Cyrus takes both daggers and throws them directly to the back of each evil demon's head causing them to fall to their deaths and away from Harris's hands. He is left wheezing and exhausted. Cyrus approaches Harris, "Are you okay, Harris?"

Harris is gasping for breath, "Yeah. I'm alright. It didn't help when they were starving."

Cyrus chuckles, "Oh come on, Harris. What did you expect? You're delicious." He yanks his daggers from their heads, "Shall we keep moving?"

Cyrus and Harris exit the mausoleum and back into the graveyard as they impale more dead evil demons on a rusted iron gate in front of the mausoleum. Cyrus lights a torch and raises his above his head as Harris complains, "This is absolutely insane. Do we really need to do this?! It's getting too much for me. This is why I hate exterminating. It just doesn't suit me."

Cyrus continues to illuminate their path, "Yeah. So let me ask you a question. Why do you do it anyway...?" Harris shrugs, "I don't know. Maybe I do it just for the fun of it." Cyrus lights the bodies on fire as they mount on to their horses. Cyrus looks at Harris, "It's nice that we are leaving a trail as we go. It's like a sign I guess."

"I guess I couldn't agree with you more, Cyrus. They'll end up making a fantastic meal for the idiots." Suddenly, they hear some howling. Harris turns back at the glaring fire they lit, "Oh shut up and enjoy your inferno. Will you?!" The Eagle swoops down and lands on Cyrus's shoulder as Cyrus and Harris ride into the fog.

Chapter 3

At a barren field, a screaming woman whose head is covered by a sack gets dragged through a field by two of Big Daddy's soldiers. Big Daddy watches her while a Priest follows her and rapidly recites the Bible passages with a small angry mob of men, women and singing children. The woman is led to a guillotine constructed on a wooden stage. Meanwhile, one of Big Daddy's soldiers, Colonel Zyrian Splatter pays money to another soldier, Vinny. Children recite in a soprano voice, "*Slay the enchantress for she is Satan's hellion. Execute her. Slaughter her and bring her remains to the inferno. And once she's barbecued, feed Satan his favourite meat.*"

Vinny speaks, "It is very much required, Colonel. This does not go unappreciated. There isn't a time when I'm not grateful to serve Satan and get rid of those fallen women for you, Sir. I'd hate to overstay my welcome but I hope it's alright for you if I hang around for the celebrations." Splatter gets clearly repulsed by Vinny as they get on the guillotine stage. Splatter looks at him, "You're more than welcome to stay just as long as you keep your distance." Vinny responds, "You're the boss, Colonel."

Splatter turns to walk up the platform steps as Vinny remarks, "By the way, Colonel. Before you do anything else, don't you have anything for me?" Splatter looks at him and remembers what he needs to do. He pulls a handkerchief wrapped object out of his pocket and gives it to Vinny. Vinny takes it, opens it and sees a dismembered finger. He smiles back to Splatter, "Thank you, Colonel. I'm delighted to hammer out deals with you as we did all the time."

Vinny walks off as Splatter watches him with a scowl. He turns and walks up the stairs as Splatter joins his right-hand man, Superintendent Officer Jackson. The soldiers drag the woman up the main steps where the hooded executioner straps her into the guillotine.

The woman struggles, she looks at her missing finger. Splatter looks at his paperwork and addresses the hushed crowd, "In the name of the master of enchantress persecution, Big Daddy Jesse Sparrow, the master's rule stated that today which is December the 24th is the day of our annual festival where we will proudly celebrate the one, we worship. And as it happens, today is that day where we found our beloved, Jenny Colane condemned for her crime of blasphemy. She had plotted and pledged against the one we all worship proudly." The crowd chants, "Enchantress! Enchantress! Enchantress! Enchantress!" The Woman screams as Officer Jackson notices a horse-drawn carriage with the flag of the Sovereign Council accompanied by two armed guards arriving. Jackson looks at it and states, "Colonel, I think the majestic carriage is on its way." "Wonderful." Splatter answers with a smug look.

He turns to the others on stage, "Right, everybody! Listen up! I need all of you to be on guard. Do you understand me?! The Chief of State is here." They see a carriage being carried towards them. Two government representatives, the State Advocate, Advocate Max Steadman and the Chief of State, Mr Michael Colane are on the carriage. Steadman and Colane look at them for a moment and then step from the carriage. Splatter steps down from the stage to greet them. Colane mentions, "Colonel Splatter, would you care to clarify to us what is happening here?" "Yes, I do, Mr Colane. I am exterminating pagans and apostates, Sir." Splatter says as he goes through his folder of papers.

Colane stands up straight and fold his arms to his chest, "I believe not, Zyrian. This is my city and I won't allow it." Steadman agrees, "That is correct. Colonel Splatter, you have disgracefully dishonoured the new law of this year where enchantress persecution is no longer allowed not only in Eagletown but in Eagle City as well. It has been banned by the new government."

Splatter steps closer to Colane, "Sir, I hate to be the bearer of bad news but I'm afraid your authority ends at this moment and at my watch...Advocate. Now if you don't mind, I got a job to do...." Splatter turns to walk back up to the stage as Steadman shouts off fumingly, "This is absolutely horrific! We can't tolerate such atrocity that involves evil and barbarism! It's a disgraceful scandal!" Colane hollers out in anger, "That's it. I've had enough. Security! And all departments of defence! I am ordering you all to detain Colonel Zyrian Splatter and place him under arrest!"

The soldiers match forward to arrest Splatter but before they can move, they abruptly get speared in the hearts with arrows and fall dead. The Chief of State and Advocate stand in shock as Big Daddy's soldiers emerge and grab them while the crowd cheers in support of this move. Splatter reveals his true colours and his allegiance alongside Big Daddy's soldiers as he returns to the stage and smiles down at The Chief of State. He stands by the sign and declares, "I really apologise, Sir....but I'm afraid we can't put up with any pagans or apostates no matter what the authority says, Sir. You need to understand that there is nobody superior to the jurisdiction of the one we worship."

Splatter rips the sack off the woman's head as Colane blurts out, "Jenny?!" Colane gazes in horror as he sees his wife screaming hysterically with a teary filled face. He looks at Splatter furiously, "Zyrian Splatter! You bastard! Let my wife go right now!" Splatter chuckles calmly, "Let her go?! You have nothing to be concerned about, Sir. I will let her go. Alright? I will let her go...."

Jenny shouts and screams away as Splatter continues his sentence, ".... from a longevity of wickedness profanity and deception!" Splatter signals to the executioner. He releases the blade while Colane panics and screams out with a mixture of shock and anguish, "Jenny! No!" Colane watches helplessly as he sees Jenny getting decapitated to her death. Her head drops down from the stage and rolls down with a thud. After killing Jenny, Splatter looks above him and an entrance emerges. He sees a semi-nude animatronics girl riding a mechanical monster at a suspended sign that reads, "MOUTH OF THE UNDERWORLD". Splatter smiles as he looks inside the walls and sees anarchy.

*

At a haunted palace, throughout the night, loud and bottom-heavy music pumps from within the palace. A flashing neon sign above reads, "THE SPOOKY MANSION" and the slogan pulses below reads, "DAMSELS, SPUNK AND ARMS". A Big-Sized Brute slams his head right into the table causing his forehead to split the nose of another thug who slumps to the ground. The crowd cheers the victor as dancing girls in tiger suits gyrate to the music on raised platforms oblivious to the violence around them.

At a Tavern Bar, Harris sits down at a table and looks at a map of a hand-drawn diagram of a building layout. He speaks to his old friend and former member of his old gang,

The Dark Rovers called Hawkins. Harris looks at Hawkins, "Oh come on, Hawkins. Don't tell me you've lost your touch."

Hawkins replies, "Don't be stupid, Harris! I don't think it's worth going at it with these idiots. I saw them killing a lot of people." Harris sarcastically critiques, "Oh my apologies. Forgive me for not trying to get to the head of state. I hope you're sure of this."

Hawkins asks, "Are you calling me a liar now? I've already told you. He's not far off. He's here. Let me show you." He points to the map, "Here we are. It's a lodging house. When you get there, ask for the labourer rancher's girl. It's in room number 24. Knowing him, he's probably in a meeting with all of his lodgers."

Harris looks keenly at the pointed spot on the map, "That's wonderful. I hope you're right.... because it seems like it's the only place on the map. It'll be a waste of time if I arrive there and find nothing." Hawkins blurts out, "Shut up, Harris! You know I'm right. I shouldn't have to convince you any further. I've already figured it out. It wasn't easy. Trust me. There is only one way in. The other way would be to climb up the side of the building." Harris chuckles and gets distracted as an unnaturally large breasted waitress passes by. Harris looks at her and giggles, "Crikey! Have you seen the beauty you got here? It's crazy."

Hawkins glimpses then and sighs, "Harris, man. This is no joke. I strongly recommend that you give it a long thought before you make any hasty decisions." Harris gets back his serious face on, "You got to understand that between Cyrus and me, those people.... the murdering sons of bitches will think back and wish they were never born."

"So, this kid you brought up? Where is he?" Harris looks around the crowd of people, "He is somewhere around here...Ah, there he is." He points to Cyrus at the bar who is enjoying the company of the dancing girls. Hawkins points ahead, "That Indian guy over there?"

Harris nods with pride, "Yep. I took him under my wing and brought him up when he appeared in my house. I had to take him in. I taught him how to fight and defend himself. His adoptive mother was killed and I couldn't just put him out on the evil streets.... not when I knew how it felt like especially when I lost my family."

Hawkins consoles him, "Sorry to hear about that." Harris takes a long and hard look at Cy, as the noise fades in the room fades in to the back ground. A million thoughts and ideas run through his mind before snapping back to reality.

"No. It's alright. He's a good kid. I realized when you look at him, you'll notice that he's not like most ordinary people but trust me when I say this...He's nothing compared to a blazing rage. He normally keeps to himself and people don't normally remember the wrath he holds...Bang! He'll come at you without thinking twice."

As they talk, two ugly goons, Teddy and Jimmy who both happen to be members of the Black Towers, walk towards Cyrus and approach him. Hawkins and Harris look on. As they watch, Hawkins suggests, "I'm not sure I understand what you're saying, Harris. You may not realize this but it could be that you and your lone wolf are underestimating those thugs. I'll be completely honest with you. The Black Towers do not know the meaning of the word, 'Heart'. It's not in their dictionary." Harris laughs maniacally, "We are no different, Hawkins. Trust me on that."

On the other side of the bar, Cyrus has his back turned to Teddy and Jimmy while he faces the bar counter. Teddy and Jimmy approach him. Teddy pokes him on the shoulder from behind. Cyrus ignores them as he does not want to draw attention to himself. Teddy starts to pick on him, "Oi! Indian!" Teddy pokes him harder but Cyrus continues to ignore him. After that, Teddy loses his patience and says, "Oi! Idiot! Are you deaf?! Or are you just plain stupid for not listening?!" Jimmy jeers at him, "Hey! Don't you realize that you're being rude, you little twerp?!"

Harris and Hawkins continue watching from a distance. They notice the predicament Cyrus is in. Hawkins states, "I think we're about to prove your point now." Harris grins and becomes supremely confident whilst he turns back to his drink.

"Why aren't you looking?"

"It's nothing I haven't seen yet, Hawkins. It gets boring over the course of time."

Cyrus slowly turns as he calmly takes a sip of his drink, "Alright, guys! What's up? Is there something I can do for you?" Teddy ridicules, "Yes. You can. You can get off my spot, Jerk-Off!"

Jimmy repeats after Teddy, "That's right, Jerk-Off. That's our spot. Now do yourself a favour and get off from our chair before we move it for you. It's reserved!" Cyrus calmly picks his drink up and takes a sip from it. Hawkins continues to watch Cyrus from a distance.

Cyrus continues to engage in an altercation with Teddy and Jimmy, "Come on, guys! I'm very thirsty and when I don't have any fuel in my body, I get very angry so, I think it would be in your best interest that you both troublemakers disappear before trouble erupts and believe me when I say this.... you don't want to get on my bad side."

Teddy sarcastically jokes, "I'm sorry. I didn't get that. What did you just say?"

"Come on. Spill it out. Tell us what you just said." Jimmy supports. He turns his head to Teddy, "Have you heard this little twerp right here?! Is he being serious or what?"

Teddy scoffs, "Yeah. I think he's got a death wish. Do you know what you've just signed up to? Your destiny!" Jimmy turns his head back to Cyrus who remains quiet as he takes his glass and drinks from it. This annoys Teddy even more. Teddy becomes angry, "I think Jimmy may be right. You have signed up to your own destiny.... because you've just signed your death warrant." Teddy whips a meat cleaver out and swings it at Cyrus but in one smooth move, Cyrus ducks, spins and draws his sword. He stabs it right through Teddy's heart, killing him instantly. Jimmy jumps back and draws his gun and fires at Cyrus but Cyrus counters it and yanks the sword back out of Teddy's heart. He uses the blade to deflect the bullets. After a round of bullets, Jimmy finds his gun empty. He panics and runs away but Cyrus throws his sword and nails at him through the back to the dancing platform.

The girl dancing above remains unfazed while she watches the chaos and feels stupidly stunned.

Harris smiles at his reaction as he finishes the last of his drink on the other side.

Chapter 4

The Delphic Fortress, a forbidding structure high atop a desolate hill. This is the home of Big Daddy, the master chamber inside is decorated with the finest comforts that money can buy. Bizarre antiques and twisted art objects clutter the room and create a chamber of horrific atmosphere. Meanwhile, across the room, the disturbing still life of young girls who resembles the brides of Dracula are arranged with a ghastly combination of props which ranges from headless bodies to crucified animals. Adding to the macabre, Big Daddy is singing serenades from Faust standing before a large canvas. Now in his 90s, he is still in his striking figure with slicked-back hair and a long Fu Manchu-style moustache and beard. He holds one of his many dark and beautiful wives, Duchess Kimmy.

In the meantime, in the Fortress hallway, Splatter walks down the long stone corridor with two masked guards in demonic armour. They are dragging a bound and gagged Colane behind them. Splatter stops at Big Daddy's imposing wooden door and knocks. After a beat, a panel in the door slides open as Kimmy stares back at Splatter with a look of disgust. The panel slaps shut and the door opens. Splatter enters into Big Daddy's chambers while the guards drag the squirming Colane before Big Daddy who remains mostly preoccupied with his wives. Splatter declares, "Big Daddy, here I am to deliver you the most righteous man to ever serve this country, Mr Michael Colane."

Big Daddy glances briefly in his direction, "Mr Colane! What a pleasure to have you here! Thanks for stopping by. I don't mean to be rude but I have errands to finish. I don't use enough time spoiling and pampering myself when these things are going on in my life." Colane stares at Big Daddy, "Jesse Sparrow, you bastard! No citizen of Eagle City is going to accept this. You're gonna burn in the fire I can tell you that!"

"Let me see. This isn't right. Is it? What could be missing from this structure?" He has his eyes fixated on a small box on a table, "Oh. Before I forget...Kim, darling. You don't mind. Do you, my sweetie-pie?" Kimmy opens the box and pulls Jenny's head out. She sets it on the display as Colane struggles to break free but find it's useless. Colane screams at Big Daddy, "You evil son of a bitch! I'm gonna murder you! I'll make sure you'll pay for this! Did you hear that?! I'm gonna make sure you'll pay for this!"

Big Daddy laughs quietly, "I get increasingly impatient from these crazy deflections. Do me a favour. Will you? Make sure you get this excruciating downer sent to Smiley. I'll come down as soon as I can. I won't be long." Splatter nods in agreement, "As you wish, Master." The Guards drag screaming Colane out of the door while Big Daddy returns to his wives with a thin smile stretching his lips, "Right. Let's pick up where we left off. Shall we...?"

At a Laboratory, opera swells throughout the night as Colane barely stays alive. He wakes up to find himself strapped to an ancient operating table in the middle of this mechanical hell with tubes and wires connected all over his body. Colane looks around him and notices that the laboratory has all the trappings filled with dark cobwebbed stone walls encasing a bizarre cluster of menacing machines and barbaric torture devices. Shortly, an old white-haired man in a lab coat, Dr Louie Smiley arrives and walks towards Colane. He inserts a small steel rod into his head. Big Daddy walks in and grins followed by his two brides with white gowns covering their heads. Big Daddy looks at Colane, "Dr Smiley, we're all set to go. Right?" Dr Smiley responds, "We are indeed, Master."

Dr Smiley steps up to the board and hits a switch which causes Colane's eyes to pop open. Colane wakes up and looks around the room. At the same time, Dr Smiley turns to Big Daddy and notices him grinning, "How are you doing, Sir? It's a lovely day. Isn't it? I hope you're okay though. It seems like you were having quite an eventful time."

Colane struggles to speak but a small metal cage holds his jaws shut. Big Daddy continues to speak to him, "I've actually been giving this a lot of thought. How should I address you again? Michael? Or shall I call you, Mick? What would you prefer to be called?"

Colane stares in horror while the brides laugh. Big Daddy goes on, "You know something? I've always been a high-class person. I don't like causing such bloopers but when I come to think of it, I asked myself why should I bother? I mean being the man I have always wanted to be, I am courageous, intelligent, brave and fearless. That's just how I see myself but don't take this the wrong way, Mick. I mean...I'm a generous guy. I'm actually a nice guy even though people think that I am an evil bastard. People are entitled to their opinions but I don't see myself that way...I'm just smart. That's all. I'm really sorry for what has happened to your wife but just so you understand, I never had the option to spare her. Instead, I had to make a meal out of her head for the hungry dogs."

Colane's eyes burn red while Big Daddy's brides continue to giggle in delight. Big Daddy continues to speak to Colane, "If it's any consolation, let me show you how much of a nice person I can be. In light of what has happened to your wife, I do feel that I should lay your law-abiding head to rest in the exact spot your wife's head is. I think that's a generous offer. Don't you think?" Dr Smiley sniggers, "There couldn't be a better offer, Big Daddy. It's the most righteous and honourable thing to do."

Big Daddy ruffles Colane's head teasingly, "I think it's time to bid our farewell, Mick. Have a safe trip to the underworld. I hope the trip will be smooth as hell." Big Daddy's brides tease him as they giggle loudly, "Have a lovely flight, Mick. Enjoy the afterlife."

"I got to admit I was actually appalled and sickened by that show of corporeal operations." Dr Smiley comments.

Big Daddy stares at Colane right in the eyes, "Get used to it." He waves at him as Dr Smiley throws another hard switch to Colane's head. This releases a surge of electric charges that rip through Colane's brain. Colane's eyes turn black and blood gushes from his mouth and eyes. An echo of Colane's horrible and violent scream before he slumps over and dies instantly, fills the lab as everyone lets out an evil laugh. They disperse as Smiley gets instructions to bag up the remains of Colane.

Big Daddy is now sitting on his throne holding Jenny's skull. He rolls a finger across the teeth. Splatter paces around holding his helmet and sipping his drink. He crosses over to the balcony. Big Daddy gets up and goes over to the balcony. He looks out over the barren countryside, "Wow! Take a look at all the wisdom of discipline. I got to admit to you that you were a gorgeous woman, Jenny. You were absolutely delicious." He then kisses the skull as Splatter turns to him, "With Michael Colane no longer a threat to us, we're gonna be unstoppable."

Big Daddy continues spinning the skull, "Trust me when I say this, pal. This was always the plan and how it was supposed to end up. I've been longing for this opportunity for very sophisticated years on end. The moment I saw the final drip of his haemoglobin clot coming from his circulator's blood loss....it delivered the whole government to beg and worship me.... only for them to get disgraced, crushed, conquered and disclosed from their true selves.... because what you saw weren't government operatives no more. They were threatened lamb traditionalists who were just waiting to be executed while they were busy dancing...."

At a desolate field, a woman called, Mackie enters. She calls to her sheep as they wander towards an evil machine pumping smoke. She is one of Big Daddy's employees who support his cause.

Big Daddy standing at the balcony, frantically works the controls above as he continues to speak to Splatter, "....and as they were busy dancing, they became oblivious of the danger ahead of them.... because they didn't know that the boss above them is governing every manoeuvre, they pull on us...."

As they continue watching her from a distance, Mackie screams at the sight of her sheep. She walks into the sheep's blood that squirts out of the machine and splashes on her. She does not seem bothered by the sight of blood.

Big Daddy continues to speak to Splatter, ".... I actually feel sorry for that tiny innocent sheep but I guess it's time to bid farewell to it...See you."

Mackie, who is still covered in blood, strips her clothes off and reveals her tail and horns. Her pet wolf arrives. Mackie and her pet wolf embrace as a silhouette of a heart forms around them.

Big Daddy and Splatter grin together on the balcony, "Now that's what I call love." He knocks the last of his drink and slams the glass.

Cyrus and Harris arrive at a lodging house's roof at night. Harris says, "Right. Here we are. We got here alright. Didn't we?" The flashing neon ahead of them illuminates the enveloping fog as Cyrus and Harris creep across the roof to a skylight while Harris refers to Hawkins's diagram. As they continue to walk, Cyrus inquires, "Are you certain that you can actually believe that weirdo you were with? I don't think I want to be strolling right into the arms of The Devil's army."

"Come on, Harris. Hawkins may be an idiot but he's not that bad. We've known each other for a very long time.... way before you even entered this world." Cyrus turns to him, "You guys go way back. Huh? Nice."

"Of course, we go way back. He's a Dark Rover, Cy. He's a good friend of mine. He won't set me up for murder. Now if he stated that those rascals are where he sent us to, then he won't be wrong I can tell you that."

"Alright then. I'll take your word for it but if I sense that we're gonna get killed, I'll just stand by those shining doorways to remind you what I've just said to you." Cyrus states.

Harris looks at him and feels thoroughly annoyed, "Let's be on guard. Shall we?" Cyrus and Harris stoop down and open the skylight up which causes the moonlight and neon to flood the dark hotel stairwell just as the skylight creaks open. Cyrus climbs down the ladder with a sawed-off shotgun in each hand. He steps down and waits for Harris. Cyrus sees the stairwell littered with empty bottles and other garbage.

He looks up at Harris as he struggles to get through the skylight. Cyrus smirks and whispers, "Let's go then. I don't know why we're waiting. Whatever...Cartilage erection...." Harris whispers back, "Sorry. I didn't get that. Say it again. They never really considered my massive cartilage erection when they made this blooming thing." Harris steps down off the ladder and draws his weapons as Cyrus shrugs, "Doesn't matter. Come on. Let's get moving. We don't have any more time to waste." This is the kind of thing that Cyrus and Harris do now. Capturing and delivering bounties. The posters that they spotted earlier was asking for Vinny and his group of friends in exchange for a hefty bounty. The work is not easy but the current times have proven they have to do anything to survive.

Cyrus and Harris make their way down the crumbling stairs to the fire door that leads to the second floor. Harris states, "Hawkins was telling me that the guy normally has a couple of lodgers protecting him." Cyrus remarks after him, "Yeah? Well, the ones that I took care of at the bar do not count which means there might be a few more of them that are responsible for this." He opens the door a crack and peeks through. He sees one of Vinny's lodgers standing guard in front of Room 24 while muted sounds of music pulse from within. Cyrus whispers, "It seems like this sucker is having an informal gathering with folk music in there." Harris tries to peek through him, "Well come on then. Tell me what you're seeing."

Cyrus, who is still looking continues to whisper, "I can see one by the door.... don't ask me anything else because that is all I can see." Harris responds, "Good. Shall we invade in and kill them? They'll be dead in no time, pal." Cyrus turns to him with a slight head turn, "Really?" "Yeah."

They spot an empty whiskey bottle by their feet. Harris looks at it, "I wonder why this is here." Cyrus smiles and steps over it, "Come on, Harris...."

Harris replies, "Oh don't you start."

Cyrus picks the empty whiskey bottle up and hands it to Harris as he says, ".... Right. Here's the plan. You ready to hear this?" Harris rolls his eyes, "No, thanks. We're not doing that crap you normally pull."

Cyrus replies in a whisper, "It's easy. First, we knock. Then we get ready and then we strike. It can't be more complicated than what I've just explained." Harris grumbles, "Alright then. I'll get you for this if you dare embarrass me."

Meanwhile, in Vinny's Room, Vinny and his lodgers' party the night away as psychedelic lights pulsate to the groove of the blaring music. The Devil's Starlets, a group of dancing girls, get in and start to dance on the tables. Everyone gets excited as they receive wolf-whistles from Vinny and his drunken lodgers. In the hallway, a lodger yells across the room, “Come on, Vinny! Show your housemates how it’s done!”

He continues to dance with a girl on his arms, “Ooh! Give me a twirl, girl!” Vinny responds to that request silently with the two-fingered salute. His lodgers stand and watch while his shotgun lays across his folded arms. He turns to look at the girls on the tables but suddenly, the fire exit door bursts open. Harris enters and stumbles out drunkenly with the whiskey bottle in one hand and keys in the other. He slurs and mutters in his hum nonsensically as he accidentally but intentionally drops the bottle. Vinny’s Lodger looks on and chuckles to himself as Harris weaves from one room to another and tries to fit his keys in each door. He moves from one door to the next stumbling and knocking things over. The people don’t mind him that much, because they think it is another drunk man who has had too much to drink.

On the other hand, Cyrus silently moves across the roof of the lodging house and stops at the edge. He looks down and hears the sounds of Vinny's party coming through the roof vibrating under his feet. The Eagle arrives and lands on the ledge outside Room 24 as the party raging inside reflects through its visionary eyes. Cyrus climbs over the edge of the roof and onto the ledge of the building.

Harris is now stumbling within fifteen feet of the lodger, “It’s freezing in here. Can you put the heating on...I paid for good service....and I want good service....” He gets almost nose to nose with the lodger who has to put his arms up to keep Harris from falling on top of him. He tries to speak to Harris, “Just hold on a second. I’ll take you to your room. We’re almost there....” Harris pretends to mumble, “The heating....”

The Lodger pushes him off, "You know what? I don't know why I'm helping you. Go and find your own room."

Harris sustains the note, ".... No...."

The Lodger lets his arm go, "Go on! Take a hike!" He falls on top of the lodger again but this time he sticks him in the gut with a knife. He makes a gurgling sound as he dies on Harris's arms just before Harris pushes him off to the side.

Cyrus draws his guns and waits on the ledge just outside the window. He witnesses everything happening in the room from a mirror's reflection on one wall.

Harris un-scrolls the wanted poster of Vinny and flattens it out. He slides it under the door and knocks hard. One of Vinny's lodgers picks the wanted poster up from the other side of the door, "Yoh, Sir! You got to see this!" He hands it to Vinny who takes it and reads from it. Vinny furiously reacts to it when he sees the words, "ROT IN HELL, YOU EVIL BASTARD!" scrawled across his face.

Harris waits with his back against the side of the wall as a hurricane of bullets rips through the door and into the opposite wall.

Cyrus bursts through the window and into Room 24 upon hearing his cue. He immediately takes two lodgers out with quick blasts from each shotgun. In the meantime, some of Vinny's lodgers stand by the front door and notice Cyrus. They turn to look at him at the window but suddenly, Harris crashes through what's left of the front door and tackles an unsuspecting lodger.

Vinny turns and fires at Harris who uses the lodger as a human shield causing an array of bullets to descend on his body. Harris fires back at Vinny who dives behind an overturned table. At the same time, the last remaining lodger fires at Cyrus but Cyrus takes a flying leap and fires back as he nails the lodger in the chest and splatters him against the wall. Cyrus bounces off the bed, flips in mid-air and lands on his feet. Suddenly, all of the four Devil's Starlets pull out swords that ignite into blue flames. They split off as two of them go to attack Harris while the other two go to attack Cyrus. Harris fires his gun away at the attacking starlets but his bullets cannot penetrate the strokes of the flaming swords. He drops his guns and draws his own sword while the starlets lunge at him. One of the starlets shouts out, "Dark Rovers will not invade here and kill us!"

Harris blocks their swords with his as all three connect with a flash of electricity. He shoves the starlets backwards as Cyrus fences off with the other pair of the starlets. Cyrus knocks one of the starlet's swords out of her grasp and flips it up into the ceiling which ignites instantly while Harris gets backed against a wall and savagely trade blow for blow with his opponents. The room gets ignited with the fallout from the flaming swords. In the meantime, spook dives and swings while Harris ducks as one of the starlets' swords lodges in the wall. Harris seizes his chance and drives his sword through her gut and kills her.

The other starlet grabs hold of Harris's sword and stumbles back. Harris grabs her flaming sword from the wall and continues fighting. Meanwhile, Cyrus, who is still fighting, jumps back and plunges his sword into her heart and kills her. One of the starlets swings at him. The starlet falls forward onto Cyrus but Cyrus kicks her back and pulls his bloody sword back out. The other starlet screams, "No!

Don't!" She leaps onto Cyrus and knocks him halfway out the window. Cyrus struggles while the starlet clings just as she tries to slash his throat. In the meantime, Vinny seizes the opportunity to flee and escapes through another window then the fire escape on to the roof. Cyrus sees him getting away and flips the starlet backwards out the window which causes her to scream and fall to her death. The room gets engulfed with fire and smoke as part of the roof gives way and crashes down on Harris and the last girl of 'The Devil's Starlets' whom Harris is still fighting with. Cyrus looks at Harris in a panic, "Harris!"

Harris emerges from the flaming debris and finds that the other starlet has been crushed to death. Harris says, "Get over here now! I'm here!"

"Go through the stairs...He's trying to get away with his speedy legs...Go on! He's on the roof!" Harris runs out of the door while Cyrus accesses the fire escape.

Harris emerges on the lodging roof from the stairwell. The Eagle watches them as Harris walks past the crooked television antenna perched on the roof. The Eagle turns its head while he walks by. Cyrus comes up the fire escape at the other end of the roof and finds Vinny is nowhere to be seen but other stairwell entries and skylights provide potential hiding places. Cyrus and Harris keep quiet and draw their guns as they search for him. The Eagle turns its head as Cyrus freezes and gets a vision through The Eagle. He sees Vinny sneaking up behind Harris from behind the stairwell entry with a gun in hand. Upon sensing danger, Cyrus quickly spins around and fires his gun directly at Harris who ducks and almost goes through the roof just as the bullet just misses the top of his head.

Harris turns around, "What in the hell are you doing, Cy? What?! You're crazy! Do you know that...?" Vinny falls on top of him and dies from a bullet to his head. Harris realizes what is has happening and is left as shocked as a bird landing on a live wire. Cyrus says, "I guess the lodging boss has just run out of luck...Everybody." Harris shoves dead Vinny off of him, "Frigging Psycho! That was a close death call!" Cyrus sarcastically blows the smoke from his gun, spins it and slides it back into his holster, "You need to forgive me on that, my friend. I was actually going down that route." Harris laughs but is still shaken, "Damn."

"Once you've finished showing gratitude to me for making sure you're alive and well, we can go and get our dosh. Right?" Harris complains, "To hell with that, you frigging psychopath."

Chapter 5

At Big Daddy's Chambers in the Fortress, Big Daddy gets sprawled out on the bed. He is being fed and pampered by Kimmy and several other brides from his Harem. Suddenly, they hear an urgent pounding at the door. Big Daddy calls out angrily, "Get that. Will you? I wonder who it is this time of the night." Kimmy goes to answers the door and a 101-year-old Eve walks in. Eve walks unsteadily, drops to her knees and cowers before Big Daddy, "Big Daddy....please forgive me but I hate to be the bearer of bad news."

Big Daddy turns to her with concern, "Eve! Why are you here? Has something happened? Tell me!" Eve replies in a weak and fragile voice, "Nothing has happened yet...Big Daddy but I do feel that I have a duty to inform you of some terrible revelation."

"Come on then. Tell me. Tell me what it is." Eve stammers, "Big Daddy...I uh.... well...." Big Daddy interrupts her due to impatience, "Oh for goodness sakes, come on you old bag! Stop stammering and tell me! The suspense is killing me and I have better things to do rather than hearing your stammer."

Eve finally responds with a shaky voice, "Your adversary is back with a vengeance upon thee." Upon hearing the news, Big Daddy cringes his face in shock as he stares at Eve.

Meanwhile across the skies, the silhouette of The Eagle flies across the full moon over The Delphic Fortress.

Big Daddy is kneeling before an altar in the gardens inside his fortress. He looks at strange forms twist together. Suddenly, slither tentacles reach out from the walls and attach themselves to his arms, face and neck. Big Daddy's face starts to burn and his eyes roll into a yellow colour. The altar transforms into a bizarre humanoid form of The Demon King. Big Daddy speaks in a strange alien tongue while he converses with The Demon King, "Your Highness, The Ruler of Hell, the ring has found an obstacle in our path. We have a rogue hunter standing between us in our hub. The shadow has returned from the realm of the underworld after serving his time on earth for a long time."

The Demon King replies in a similar dialect but deeper, "You are right. Your enemy has returned with nothing but revenge in his mind." Big Daddy gets startled, "But it's impossible. How did he manage to come back after I trapped him in the cage of death?"

"It was never going to be easy for you. With every ounce of effort, you've worked for, no attack of yours is capable to fool the written destiny you've signed up for. It'll only make your enemy mightier formidable than he already is. Through the fire and gore, your covenant deal has already been closed and here we are now, as we stand before each other, his fate lies in you and your fate lies in his." Big Daddy suddenly becomes restless, "And how can I crush my immortal enemy? How do I exterminate God's Guardian Cherub who has already died and cannot be killed again?"

"That's where you are wrong. There is always a way to kill death. I shall put my trust on The Heavy Hammer to collect his soul and personally send it to me. I will then devour his supernatural spirit. The others will come after," he replies.

"I'll arrange for it. You won't be disappointed, Your Highness."

At a mortuary office, the lifeless body of Vinny lies on a cold metal table. His eyes are open and frozen in a death grin. A hand reaches in and sticks a finger into the bullet hole in his forehead. Alongside Vinny, the bodies of Vinny's lodgers and the four Devil's Starlets are propped against a wall of severed heads encased in glass. A feeble old man in a wheelchair and a body collector called, Spence check the identity of each body against the wanted poster pictures as Cyrus and Harris stand nearby. Cyrus looks around and sees a wall packed with wanted posters while Spence's huge and well-armed brute of an assistant keeps an eye on them. After a long stare at them he goes into a back room.

Spence remarks, "Praise to the Lord! This is how it's done. This is how we slay the bloodhounds. You must be proud of that. They are all executed and have paid for their crimes. Blooming heck! Both of you must have had the guts to slay these evil bastards and....bitches. I never thought that would happen."

"To be honest with you, those evildoers were just sudden extra thunderbolts that we never negotiated for," Harry articulates as he continues staring at the posters on the wall. "Come on, Spence. Stop being a sponger and do some work. I need somebody in these bags before the entire office starts to smell." The body collector swings with his chair to one of the girls, "Howling! If there was a slight chance, this bitch will be mine on the other side of my king size bed. I can imagine how dirty she will be...." Harris steps up to collect while the body collector looks up and smiles, "You know I was only joking. Right? I don't put professionalism and personal blissful satisfaction all into one bowl and stir it all up together. Anyway, I think I owe you both some dosh."

Harris nods in agreement as he rests his hands on his waist, "Yeah? I think a hundred thousand should be correct...not to mention, an extra forty for the girls." Spence points a gloved finger to him in agreement, "And that totals one hundred and forty. Doesn't it?" He turns and slides open a metal gate and rolls his chair inside and closes the gate behind him.

Harris asks, "Okay. You got it. So, if I may ask, whose idea was this?" Spence responds, "Your guess is as good as mine. I only know what you know. I'm not going to lie to you. Vinny did have many enemies watching him if I'm going to be honest with you." He opens a safe and continues, "A while back, I would have done it on my own. The problem is...I got shot but never mind. That's in the past. We can't expect anything much from this God-Forsaken earth that we're living in. We're living in a world where we have to put up with all the terrors that are happening around us. Back in the day, we never heard people shouting from all this ridiculous stuff. It's all a farce."

Spence returns and starts stuffing the bodies into black bags. Harris turns to Cyrus who is still scanning the wanted posters, "Nothing useful. Right?" Cyrus responds with a frown, "I don't think so. It's a load of crap. It's doesn't even make sense."

A minute later, Spence returns with four sacks of gold coins, "There you are. There's your one hundred and forty grand like we agreed. As the motto goes...." The body collector hands the sacks over, ".... money is not the most important thing in the world. Love is but it's just fortunate that people happen to love money." He hands the two bags to Cyrus and they start heading out just as Spence's assistant pushes Spence's wheelchair up to the door to see them off. Spence calls out, "Hold up for a moment. Do any of you two want to be involved in some underground fight exhibition? I have a friend who can get us access to the drama and it's Superfluous. Think about it. People love to make money out of murder in there."

Cyrus and Harris exchange grins with each other as they exit. The body collector watches them go. Spence's assistant shuts the door. After Cyrus and Harris leave, a gunshot suddenly rings out. Spence sees his assistant toppling over onto him with a hole in the back of his head. He becomes stunned and shoves Spence off of him. Spence spins around to face a man stepping out of the shadows of the back room. He looks at the man and stunned, "The hell is going on...? I've done whatever you've ordered me to do!" The Man steps into the light and reveals himself as Splatter, "Oh. I am very thankful for it. You've been of great help. It's just too bad you have to go." He shoots Spence in the head as the impact knocks him and his wheelchair over onto its back dead. Splatter sighs, "Stupid immobilized moron."

At a deadwood back road, Cyrus and Harris ride their horses at a slow pace along a path as the light fades in a distance behind them. They burst into laughter as Harris pulls off his alcohol bottle, "Crikey! I think it's fair to say we're in luck right now, Cyrus." Cyrus glances at him, "I'd strongly recommend that you remain as alert as you can this time,

Harris. It seems to me that you're becoming more of an arrogant git like you've been in your prime."

Harris notes, "Well you need to understand something. The people over here in the woods are just frigging hillbillies and well-besieged hard cases."

"Can I have a drink of that please?" Cyrus says as he points to the bottle.

Harris throws Cyrus the bottle and Cyrus catches it, "You know something? Not everything is as it seems. You know?" Cyrus gulps down the rest of the bottle as Harris states, "Oh Come on now!"

Cyrus swallows as he grins, "Relax, man. Will you? It's for your benefit. I was only saving you.... for your own well-being." He chucks the empty bottle back at Harris, "In case you've forgotten, I was the one who brought you up after your resurrection which means I've been looking after you dutifully and if I am capable of doing that, I'll tell you something else. I am able to take care of myself and that does not include any assistance from you!"

Harris throws the bottle to the ground and shatters it. Suddenly, unbeknownst to Cyrus and Harris, an old scraggly man, Dr Sam Wayne appears and watches them from high in the trees. Cyrus and Harris's voices are heard although it is from a muted distance. They continue to talk to each other as Harris continues, "Anyway, why do you look so concerned? The plan is to just go in and take care of business before we head out again. We got to be careful because it sounds very simple but it's very dangerous."

Cyrus responds, "I'm not bothered about the place. It just feels like certain areas are beyond abnormal. I can sense what's about to happen."

Harris turns to him, "Come on, Cy. Do you want to know what I think?"

"No but I'm sure you're gonna tell me anyway."

"Okay. I reckon you're an overly suspicious lame brain. You think negative of everything pretty quickly. You wanna know something else?" Cyrus seems annoyed, "No. That's enough, Harris. Just keep that trap shut for now. Yeah? You've said it all before and it'll get a bit boring to hear you say it...." Harris reacts, "Just chill, man. Will you? Look at me first. Remember the story I told you about a former Dark Rover who turned on us?"

"Yeah. He shot you. Right?"

"No. He almost did. The bullet went past my head before I beat the crap out of him. Do you still see me looking back at my past? No. It's because it's pointless. I don't even think about my family much. After they died, I moved on, Cyrus. I took the next step by pressing on. I'm sorry about your mother but I think it's about time you did too."

Cyrus gets silent for a while, "I do appreciate everything you've done for me, Harris. You gave me some terrific theoretical advice but I wished it was easier than that."

"Well why can't it be easy?"

"It can't be easy, Harris....especially not in the situation we're in." Cyrus responds with a sombre mood. Harris picks up on the seriousness of his tone, "Come on, Cy. Just tell me. Talk to me. Maybe I can help." Cyrus enunciates, "I don't think this is the time or place for me to tell you.... it's just that everything seems like an opposed mystery supernatural force from the past is haunting me at every step of the way." He looks at Harris and sees his cringe look. Cyrus continues, "Don't worry about it. Just pretend I never said that. I know what I've just said was nonsensical."

Harris hiccups then turns serious, "I think you need to stop grieving and let me think for you. That'll be easier. Don't you think?" He pulls another bottle out and winks at Cyrus as he takes a swig. Cyrus smiles and shakes his head while they ride on ahead away at a faster pace. Meanwhile, in the trees, Dr Wayne watches them ride around the bend.

Chapter 6

At Superfluous, Cyrus and Harris ride up and dismount. They tie off their horses and head inside the underground fighting exhibition. Following this, Harris flips a coin to the doorman. Simultaneously, Splatter also arrives at the underground fighting exhibition yelling, "Hey! Keep an eye on your steps, Moron." He enters the stadium as Wayne glares at him. Splatter sees an ancient dilapidated stadium set up like something akin to a big top tent. He also sees some old sideshow posters adorning the crumbling facade, advertising past and future events. One of them which reads, 'TODAY'S EVENT WILL PRESENT THE MAIN EVENT OF THE EVENING: WELCOME EVERYBODY TO THE BRUTE OF COMBAT UNDERGROUND FIGHTING EXHIBITION!'

Dr Wayne follows in and whilst he is on his way in, he bumps into Splatter who shoves him backwards and Wayne lands on his gluteus. Splatter gets flanked by two huge guards as he realizes that he is in a dangerous mixture of a circus sideshow and theatre. Drunken patrons arrive to watch the show and they see challengers battling against the army of genetic mutants in the savage sport of underground fighting. Splatter looks around and notices that he is in a cramped arena alive with excitement and filled with ear-splitting volume of the distorted disco music and the blood-splattering action in the underground. Meanwhile, a strange sight of a part man and part machine called Dr Storm gets lowered from the ceiling to a stop just above the underground. He scans the crowd from within a mangle of rusted metal, tubes and wires as his electronic amplified voice blasts through the arena, "Welcome to my territory, ladies and gentlemen! You're all in the territory of genetic wickedness! A territory full of fanatical maniacs, nerdy weirdoes and iconoclastic prodigies! Here I am about to present you all the...."

In the meantime, through the crowds, while Dr Storm continues to speak, Cyrus and Harris push their way through the rowdy ringside crowd surrounding the underground as Harris shouts, "What was that number again?"

Cyrus asks, "What number?" Harris replies, "The one you got from them."

"Seven."

"Oh, I hate that number. Seven has always been an unlucky number for me. I don't like the feeling of this." Cyrus grins, "I thought you said to be calm."

"Don't get cheeky or over-confident with me. We're actually going round in circles in case you hadn't noticed." "No. We're not. Come on. We need to get a drink first and then check out the fights."

Elsewhere at the bleachers, Dr Wayne takes a seat as Dr Storm continues his speech, "The beautiful pulverised cinders of one mandible on top of another.

Not to mention, the swarms and the murderers are all set to demonstrate their talent. From the fanaticism mania, they originate before arriving at this arena....to raze and hound the scream I give you all...." As Dr Storm continues to speak, evil whispers surround them, "The show of superfluous." As they head off, Splatter and his two men move into the stands several rows behind them.

A fight erupts in the underground fighting pits. Two huge brutes, one human and one half-ape, half-man mutant hammer away on each other. The human brute swings his battle hammer and knocks the ape-man out cold. The scoreboard on the bleachers reads, 'SIX'.

Another fight erupts in the pits as the previous fighters are drugged from the pits. Four tiny undead creatures circle their giant hunchback opponent as they grin and expose jagged metal teeth. They leap onto the giant all at once and dig fast into his flesh but the giant tries to throw them off while their teeth find major arteries and cut through them. This cause blood to squirt out as he stumbles to his knees before he falls flat on his face to his death. The scoreboard now reads, 'SEVEN'.

At the holding cell leading to the pit, Cyrus and Harris stand behind a massive iron gate as Harris states, "Beat this idiot mercilessly so that he is not able to wake up and remember what happened to him. But be sure to have your eye on those candy throwers. I can assure you that they'll eat your eyes out of your face." Cyrus gulps his drink to the last bit before he goes in to help him keeps his calm.

Outside the cell, Dr Storm is heard announcing the next battle, "Dark blemishes and flustered, our entire universe seeks nastiness....and spontaneous cover-ups, ladies and gentlemen, please join me as we all send my wits over the edge and start the submersion.... which is number.... seven." Suddenly, the gates open and Dr Storm gets whisked back up to the rafters.

Inside the underground pits, stands a seven-foot-tall hideously deformed monster called, The Heavy Hammer. He arrives and shows his big muscular arms that are sprouting from his hunched back. He also shows his thick, powerful legs off along with his heavily stitched and bandaged body. After the crowd uproar, Cyrus emerges at the other end of the pit and finishes his drink. He throws the glass down to the floor and rubs his hands together in anticipation while he moves into square off. Suddenly, the siren rings and Cyrus draws his sword and comes out swinging. The Heavy Hammer counters by firing squirming tentacles from his arms which wraps around Cyrus and pulls him towards his gaping red jaws. He bites into his flesh before sucking Cyrus's blood out.

Eve and a small bevy of witches are at The Delphic Fortress in the meantime. They are sitting around a television screen in a semi-circle. They are all attached to an electrical device that powers it. Big Daddy is sitting in an elaborate chair as he watches the spectacular fight on a television screen. Upon recognizing Cyrus on the television screen, Big Daddy examines and utters, "I think that has to be him! There! We've got him! Now focus on him! Make sure we don't lose!" The Witches chant and moan as they desperately try to hold onto the image. Big Daddy stares at the television screen and watches Cyrus chopping at The Heavy Hammer's tentacles.

The huge jaws of The Heavy Hammer snap at Cyrus as the fighter tries to deliver the death strike but Cyrus plunges his sword deep into his gaping wound and skewers him. The Heavy Hammer's gaping wound widens and swallows Cyrus's arm as his skin sizzles from the acid. Cyrus manages to jerk his arm free and slashes his sword at the fighter again but the quivering mass of flesh envelops him and pulls him even closer.

Harris watches in amazement at the surreal scene unfolding before him. The crowd goes wild as Harris starts to worry.

At the Witches lair, the flickering image of the fight onscreen dances across Big Daddy's cackling face, "Did you see him?! What an idiot! Who in their right mind is stupid enough to just stroll into the arms of a deadly ploy especially when it is set up by me...?" He yells at the television screen, "Oh for crying out loud! You godless worm?! You're a nobody. Do you know that?! You're not even a ghost! You're a nobody!"

As he continues to watch the fight on the television screen, Big Daddy sees The Heavy Hammer's mouth expanding as the fighter begins to swallow Cyrus's entire struggling body. Big Daddy rejoices and cheers the fighter on, "Nutrition from The Almighty himself. Yeah? That's good. Eat well and absorb that idiot! Macerate him really good."

Cyrus gets almost completely engulfed by The Heavy Hammer who has doubled his size. He realizes he is now in real danger, but being the warrior that he is, he does not give up.

Splatter, who is watching from the bleachers, grins and gets up to leave as Wayne shakes his head.

Harris screams in horror, "Cy! No!" He desperately tries to find a way down into the pit to help Cyrus but Security Guards in riot-type gear stop him.

Cyrus gets completely devoured by The Heavy Hammer's body; the crowd goes wild while Dr Storm starts his descent to declare The Heavy Hammer as the winner. Cyrus is trapped against the glowing and undulating walls of flesh and the dripping acid walls burn his skin and melt his skin like wax inside Heavy Hammer's body. The walls of flesh expand into a long tunnel as a light vortex swirl at the end of the walls. Cyrus stumbles towards it but finds it struggling as he gets hit by an electrical charge from the flesh walls with each step. Each jolt triggers memories for Cyrus and Cyrus remembers himself as a little boy standing with his adoptive mother, Mrs Eagleman at his adoptive father's funeral. Cyrus remembers the masked murderer shooting Mrs Eagleman to her death. He also remembers the closing moments of his death when Big

Daddy killed him. His memory then switches to his resurrection when he was reincarnated by The Eagle and emerged from his grave thirty years ago.

As the visions cross and run through his mind, Cyrus struggles, screams and scratches his way to the light. Suddenly, tears stream from his eyes and down his face as the horrific revelations continues. Cyrus gets a new flood of imagery bombarding him when he sees chaotic scenes of people getting burnt, hanged and beheaded. He envisions the screaming tortured faces of the victims and the masked murderer from Cyrus's childhood memory standing high above the smoke with fire.

Suddenly, the voices in his head stop and he sees the masked murderer removing his mask to reveal a real devil. He sees him laughing maniacally in his house holding a gun directly at him. He sees him firing the gun at Mrs Eagleman and him. Cyrus's flashing memories stop and he drops to his knees as he strives to reach the light but it seems impossibly far away. Suddenly, the shape of an angel appears within the light and transforms into a luminous eagle. Cyrus struggles to his feet with a determined scream as The Eagle flies towards him. He reaches for it and takes hold of its talons. There is a tremendous burst of light when Cyrus and The Eagle become one. Like a strike of lightning, the inner fleshy walls of The Heavy Hammer collapse in on him.

Big Daddy watches The Heavy Hammer belch on the television screen as Cyrus disappears. He sees Dr Storm announcing victory for the fighter as he smiles victoriously before getting up to leave, "A lot of expectations for the revival of God's new Champion. I've murdered him once and I'm not afraid to do it once more." He turns to leave but Eve stops him, "Big Daddy! Look!" Big Daddy exclaims, "What?" He sees Eve still looking at the television screen. Big Daddy looks back at the screen and sees the fighter convulsing violently.

In a trice, Cyrus explodes out of the monstrous body and lets a terrible roar out as he shoots into the air and the crowd freaks out.

Splatter watches in shock as he cannot believe his eyes. His face blanches while he and his men quickly exit Superfluous.

Harris looks ahead through the metal bars of the entry gate in amazement. He could not believe Cyrus is alive, he felt like he was dreaming. The crowd goes silent for a second then an uproar of rejoicing fills the air. He realises his eyes are not fooling him and whoops in joy.

Wayne is also amazed as he continues to stare in disbelief. He quietly nods his head as the victory seems vital to him.

At a barren countryside, the sky turns darker as the full moon shimmers and gets half-obscured by black clouds. The Eagle flies across and descends on a solitary building on a desolate patch of land with a small country motel. It has a sign swinging on the creaky chains out front that reads, 'THE HELLION'S MOTEL'. It is displayed in a crude painted vampire with bat wings framing the letters.

In a dark corner of the crowded motel, Cyrus and Harris are having their dinner. They are seated by a miniature casket-shaped table with the top made of glass so anyone can see the tiny corpse inside. After they finish their huge meal, they leave the table with empty glasses, plates and bowls. Cyrus sips his drink as Harris says, "Shall we start talking? Come on. Let's talk. Just explain to me what you saw or remember.... whatever! Did you happen to see what your murderer looked like? Come on, Cy. Tell me. Talk to me." Cyrus responds, "The only memory I can think of at the moment was when I stood by my father's grave at the graveyard. There was a downpour and it washed his grave."

"Okay. Is there anything else you saw?"

"I remember my mum was pointing her finger to the stars where a big black eagle was circling over us. It was very difficult to look at it because the rain was obscuring my eyesight. My mother told me not to be afraid because The Eagle was only there to carry my father's spirit to the otherworld...." Cyrus gets up from his seat as he sees the decor of murals and coffin-shaped furniture. The Eagle lands on top of the sign outside as its head jerks toward the motel.

As Cyrus looks at everything around him, he continues to speak to Harris, ".... she also told me that my father will be waiting for us to reunite with him up in the heavens. I knew my mother got to heaven but I didn't." Harris stares at him and takes a long pull off a bottle of brew as he is troubled by Cyrus's entire story. He looks at Cyrus, "I hope these memories are not mere hallucinations, Cy. Something tells me that you're going crazy remembering all that crap. It happens a lot especially after people have been engulfed by a frigging monster." Cyrus answers, "And you have no idea how crazy it sounds? If you had known more about my first life, you'd see that my second life with your upbringing was not comparable to my first. No disrespect, Harris. I do appreciate everything you have done for me but unfortunately, it's an untaught state. I know everything now. Every move that we make is like a game of chess and everything is coming together. I know it all, Harris."

Harris stares at him blankly, "I'm not even going to listen to it. It's a lot of nonsense. If something hit your head hard, trust me when I say this.... your head hallucinates.... people see a lot of stuff.... they see their afterlife after near death experiences." Cyrus insists, "Harris, I'm not playing around with you. I've told you.... I've met my death....and you knew about that when you took me in after my reincarnation." He drinks from his glass, "I still belong to the otherworld." Harris tries to ignore what he is saying, "You're a great actor, Cyrus. I can't believe that you sat here with me dauntlessly and talked a lot of nonsense that I have to put up with all these years."

Cyrus goes on, "Harris, just listen to me. We can both agree that I'm not some sort of a slumber rider moving through the cemetery. Right? I'm a lot more than that.... a lot more than you can imagine." Suddenly, Cyrus abruptly draws his knife and stabs it through his own hand and nails it to the table. Harris sees it and jumps back in shock, "Oh God! What in the hell...!"

Cyrus stares at him calmly and painlessly before he pulls the knife out. He holds his gashed hand up and shows it to Harris who sees the wound healing itself and disappearing within moments as Cyrus says, "See for yourself. As you can see, I don't have any lesions from the green dragon's rages at all." Harris continues to stare in disbelief and blinks and slumps back into his seat, "Oh God. Crikey! I think I'm going to get another drink." Harris takes a long stare at his hand curiously while he watches it burn with the cigar and heal repeatedly. Harris says, "I'll be quite honest with you. I've always known that you were trouble the moment I saw you in my house...You took me to the cemetery to find out who you were and where you arrived from but in the end, we found nothing. Good job I took you in because I didn't want to see you dead. Now do me a favour and stop that crap. It's disgusting." Cyrus finally throws in the towel, "Oops. My apologies."

The Eagle lands in the window next to Harris as it stares at Cyrus. Harris watches Cyrus staring back as Cyrus and The Eagle sense their unique connection. Harris comments, "Maybe your mother was correct...about The Eagle I mean. Maybe it does carry the soul of the dead ones to the otherworld."

Cyrus continues to make eye contact, "Now why would I have an urge to disbelieve it?"

"So, your killer? Did you happen to see him? Who was he?"

"I'm afraid I can't answer that question at this point, Harris. I can't remember what he looks like. Maybe I couldn't see his face. I really don't know but I'll tell you something else. I still remember his evil voice."

A wave of pain fills him to the brim as he remembers the sequence of events leading up to his death, "I know he is still around somewhere in this world. The reason that eagle brought me back to earth is for one purpose and one purpose only....and that is to avenge our deaths and there is no stopping me in this universe. Nobody will be able to stand in my way." Harris raises his glass, "Okay, Cyrus. No matter what happens, I'm with you all the way." Cyrus turns to him, "Thanks, Harris. It means a lot." Harris queries with concern, "Well where do we go from here? We need to start somewhere or someone." They toast and drink as Dr Wayne sits in the booth directly behind them.

Chapter 7

Big Daddy is walking into his garden and once again transforms into the bizarre humanoid form of The Demon King at The Delphic Fortress. He re-connects himself with the real Demon King and convulses with him, "The Heavy Hammer was unsuccessful." The Demon King replies in a deep echo voice as usual, "What are you talking about?"

"This means that our arch rival is alive and well. What about his powers? The supernatural force he possesses! Will it get more powerful than it is now?" The Demon King continues, "His powers are undeniably unstoppable and will continue to grow. It's nothing we have control over for now. Your enemy has formed a connection with the soullessness from the otherworld. He holds the key to torment the afterlife just like how a mouse would do to a cat." Big Daddy becomes weary, "Then tell me! Tell me how I can prevent his steps from crossing my territory and everything I have worked hard for."

"I'm afraid that is impossible. Your enemy is on his way and he cannot be defeated or conquered. His footsteps lie on the holy soil." Big Daddy starts to be desperate and worried, "There must be a way. How do I stop him?" The Demon King goes on, "There is something you can do but you'll need to do it quickly before it's too late. You need to set a trap for your enemy within the boundaries of your fortress. The way you'll need to do it is by bringing the one who brought him up from his second birth and everything will fall back in place."

Big Daddy smiles with relief because it now seems like all hope is not lost, "The one who brought him up from his second birth. What is he called?" The Demon King goes silent for a while then with a gush of whisper, it declares, "Harris."

Cyrus is at the graveyard standing next to a tombstone. He remembers himself as a youngster when he was brought back from death and wandered in the rain feeling cold and dirty wearing the suit he was buried in. The Eagle lands on a tombstone and calls out to Cyrus. Cyrus stumbles towards The Eagle but The Eagle takes flight and flies and darts like a bullet straight up into the rainy night sky and hits its apex which is encircled by a full moon. The clouds start to part as the stars emerge and The Eagle descends back to the graveyard and swoops down to land on the shoulder of the adult Cyrus. He sits atop a tall monument that is perched high above the rest of the cemetery while he is deep in thought. As the distant lights of The Hellion's Motel become visible in the valley below, Cyrus sees himself in a different graveyard than the one he was wandering through in his childhood. He sees the graveyard being decrepit as it crumbles and gets backdropped by the ruins of an old, fire-ravaged town. Cyrus hops off the tall monument and lands with the grace of a cat while The Eagle takes flight and heads back toward the valley and watches it go.

Meanwhile through the dark woods, Splatter and a dozen army of masked guards from Big Daddy's fortress ride on horses towards The Hellion's Motel.

Harris sits at the same table at The Hellion's Motel in the back and devours yet another main course from a beautiful barmaid who delivers a steaming plate of food to him. Harris smiles at the barmaid and says, "Crikey! I think I have already had a trip to the otherworld. This food is splendid." The Barmaid flirts with Harris, "Hey, Handsome. Why don't you reveal to me if you're a brawler or sweetheart?" Harris lifts the lid to his plate of food, "I think you'll find that I'm a lot of things, Gorgeous...I am so many things more than you can ever dream of." The barmaid giggles as she gets an impish gleam in her eye. She takes her room key out and leaves it on the table, "Well I brawl really well in the bedroom. Don't you like it when a woman is rough? I tell you what. Why don't you come with me upstairs and I'll show you what you are missing out on?"

While the barmaid walks away, she winks at Harris who can hardly believe this is happening. He goes double-time on his food and hardly bothers to chew the food as he gulps it down. Suddenly, he stops when Splatter and the guards arrive bursting in but they do not see Harris among the dense crowd. Although Harris sees them, he ducks down to avoid being recognized. Splatter and the guards start to shove patrons around and ask questions. Harris mumbles to himself, "Oh my God. It's the enchantress persecutors...."

He discretely pulls his hood over his head and eyeballs the back stairway. He makes his move as a tussle breaks out with the motel owner when Splatter orders his guards, "Go find the barmaid filth and get her before me." He stops at the stairs upon hearing a scream. Splatter turns back and sees the brave patron dead on the floor with a sword in his back while two of Splatter's guards hold the barmaid hostage for Splatter to torment. While Harris looks on, he curses himself, "God, no...." Splatter draws a dagger when he moves in on the barmaid. He looks at her, "Now if this slag wants to tell me that she is clueless about what I want to know, I'm not going to buy it because she ought to know every single peasant that has served in this place. Now we're on a manhunt for a pagan by the name of Harris. He is wanted for the murder of twelve enchantress persecutors. Now come on. Talk and do it fast because I haven't got all day to check the entire place. Don't mess around because I'll only give you five seconds to tell me where he is.... or else your soul will be the last ever thing that stays on this God-Forsaken earth." She trembles like a twig on a tree on a windy day when he puts the blade to her throat and threatens her, "One...Two...Three...Four...Five...."

Before Splatter could kill her, Harris appears behind Splatter with a bang, "Wait. You're looking for me? Well, here I am." Splatter turns around to find Harris standing with his sword drawn on the stairs as shouts, "Alright, Guys. Get that piece of garbage in your cuffs. We need to detain him!" The Guards move in as Harris lets a war cry out and whirls his sword like a dervish.

Wayne creeps up at the graveyard and moves through the crumbling tombstones to follow Cyrus. He moves in delicate footsteps and breathes nervously and softly. Wayne goes behind an eroded statue of a praying angel and loses sight of Cyrus in an instant. He peers out from behind the statue and becomes bewildered as there is nowhere Cyrus could have hidden so quickly. Suddenly, he hears a gun cocked just behind him and turns around to see Cyrus holding a gun to his head. Wayne freezes as Cyrus addresses him, "Hi. Can I help you with anything?" Wayne remains glued to the ground, "Oh my God! Cyrus!"

"Surprised?"

Wayne raises his hands as an indication of his surrender, "Woah! No! I mean...Yes. Cyrus, please. Don't pull the trigger on me. Please don't kill me. I only came here for the worship. I don't have any funny business around here. Please." Cyrus pins the barrel of the gun behind his head, "I do not want to hear any of that. Now tell me who you are, what you want from me and how you know my name." Wayne replies hysterically, "Okay. I'll tell you who I am. I'm Dr Sam Wayne."

Cyrus pins the barrel harder on him as he lets out a frightened cry, "That doesn't mean anything to me, Dr Wayne. What I'm more interested in is why you were sneaking up on me in a place like this. Don't you think it's a little bit creepy?" Wayne responds, "Okay. Yes, you got me. If I'll be honest with you, you're right. I'm not going to lie to you, I was following you but it's not how you're thinking it right now. The reason I was following you is that I had to make sure that no one was following you." Cyrus seems confused, "Yeah? And why is that? Who are you? Some sort of a guardian angel?"

Wayne continues to explain, "No. I'm only here to help you kill Big Daddy Jesse Sparrow." Cyrus pauses at the mention of his name as something about it gives him an uneasy feeling but he isn't sure why. He becomes more confused, "Who the hell is that?" Wayne seems to be calmer now, "The master of enchantress persecution from The Delphic Fortress."

"Oh, Dr Wayne. If I got to admit to myself, I'd say that you are sure as hell got a lot of money than the poor state you look. You'll definitely have your place in paradise if God chooses to acknowledge the good deeds you have. Anyway, how much am I worth for your hit?" Wayne tries to insist, "You're not worth anything. I'm not hired or paid to carry out a contract killing." Cyrus laughs sarcastically, "Listen to me, Dr Wayne. I'm not stupid. I know in this era there is no one who is doing anything for free! And just to let you know, I'm gonna find an enchantress persecutor and kill him, I can assure you that it's not exactly your cup of tea so, I do not know why you want to help me." Wayne turns slightly to address him through his side, "Cyrus, you got your supernatural strength...I saw it with my own eyes. You can win this because the battle has just begun and we can only rely on you to save us."

"I do apologize but I think you'll find out that I have been in a lot of trouble myself. I have dealt with a lot of criminals and I do not want your help for now. See you." Cyrus holsters his gun and starts walking away while Wayne's face falls. Wayne moves in front of Cyrus and falls to his knees. He begs and shouts out, "Come on, Cyrus...Please...I'm begging you to please aid us in this battle." Cyrus looks down at Wayne as he gets troubled by his sheer desperation which becomes unclear what he is thinking but suddenly, he gets an eagle vision and receives a flash vision of Harris being overwhelmed by Splatter and the guards in The Hellion's Motel. Cyrus runs off and goes for his horse without another word as Wayne gets up and goes hobbling after him. Wayne shouts after Cyrus, "Hold up!"

Cyrus rides at full gallop past the wasteland as intermittent visions of Harris's bloody battle flash through his mind. In a blink of an eye, Cyrus arrives at The Hellion's Motel and sees that everything appears to be quiet. He jumps off his horse with his gun in hand and runs to the door. He kicks the door open and freezes in shock while The Eagle flutters to rest on his shoulder. Cyrus sees a gruesome scene of carnage and the patrons brutally slaughtered stringing from the rafters. Cyrus gets transfixed by the horror when he receives quick violent flashes of the slaughter that has transpired. He enters and runs up the stairs. On reaching the top, he finds a corpse that comes swinging out of the darkness. Cyrus dodges it and continues to run-up to the second floor where he kicks Harris's room door open, only to find a bloody corpse tarred, feathered and spiked to the wall. While Cyrus ponders worriedly about Harris, he finds a note nailed to the corpse's head.

He approaches in horror and terrified that it might be Harris but gets relieved for a moment when he finds that the man is not Harris. Cyrus yanks the note off and reads it, "*As the towers collapse, so did the heavy one; the darkness has arrived suddenly, as hell's victims foretell; Real agony and grief's circle becomes very visible; the sharp jaws are all that can be heard; For he has taken your name in his tongue with his thin powerless pant; I am his God, the ruler of hell; The Grim Reaper from the otherworld, I take charge of its throne; For his essence and spirit breeds emotionlessly in before me.*" After reading this note, Cyrus realizes that he has been set up. He then drops the note and stands there with a beat trembling with rage. After that, he turns and heads out with a vengeance while he still holds the note and emerges from the motel. As he exits, he sees Wayne waiting on his horse. Cyrus charges up and grabs Wayne off his horse and throttles him to the ground. He puts his hand around his neck, "You lured me into this trap! Now, where is Harris?!" Wayne replies amidst the choking, "I never...I can't tell you where Harris is...I don't know...if I can guess correctly, he's probably been dragged to the fortress."

Cyrus continues chocking him harder, "The fortress? Why? Why have they taken him there and why would they? What exactly do they want from him?" Wayne struggles to respond, "It's not him they want, Cyrus. It's you...." Wayne chokes further and starts to lose his breathe, "Please....let me go...I need to...I need to let the air out." Cyrus releases his grip but keeps the gun to Wayne, "Why me? Where do I come into their play?"

"Cyrus, you are a major danger to them."

"I don't understand. You need to explain it to me clearly. Why am I a danger to them? What is it that they want from me?" Wayne continues to plead, "I wished I knew the answers you were looking for but I honestly don't know...Come on. Let me get up. I'll take you up to the fortress. Let me take you to the site and I'll do my level best to give you all the answers that you are looking for. I'll try to tell you everything I know. Please...Please give me a chance to explain it to you. After that, if you want to kill me, you're more than welcome to."

"Okay. I guess you've just saved yourself this once but I hope this is not a goose chase. For your sake, I pray that you win because my hands are a little bit itchy at the moment which essentially means at any time, I can just pull the trigger without any hesitation and send your head across from here. Do you understand?" Wayne nods vigorously with teary eyes, "I understand." Cyrus ties him up and leads him along by a rope leash. Over the Skies, The Eagle flies through the clouds over the wastelands.

Cyrus and Wayne ride through a dark forest. They approach a gipsy wagon parked in a clearing in the woods. They see a full-on rambling roadshow and the type of rig from a carnival with a banner draped over one side reading, 'DR. WAYNE'S NOMADIC PHENOMENAL CARRIAGE'. They walk past two big Clydesdales reigning to a tree with munching on the grass and the barrel of a shotgun shoved through a small opening in one of the windows. Cyrus steps out from the shadows with a gun against Wayne's head as the shotgun gets withdrawn from the window. Suddenly, a large man haggard with tanned and leathery skin in his forties, Hunter Logan appears in the doorway and suspiciously looks at Cyrus from his gun sites. He wonders what Cyrus and Wayne are up to. He goes up to them and draws his shotgun with his hand ready on the trigger, "Wait! Stop where you are and don't move a muscle!"

Wayne freezes and lets out a squeaking voice, "Calm down, Logan. Please don't do anything stupid. It's just me and of course.... I've made a new pal over here." Logan, a man who is has been known to not be messed with his fully bearded face completing his scary look. He responds, "That's the guy. Huh?" Wayne giggles a bit to calm the situation then continues, "Of course. Here he is but unluckily, we had a bit of altercation upon our arrival here."

Logan grips the gun firmly, "And what was the altercation about, if I may ask?" Cyrus finally utters, "What I wanted to know is what Dr Wayne could not answer me. Why me?"

Wayne continues, "It seems that our new pal here, Cyrus, actually had the idea that we're Zyrian Splatter's cronies." Logan starts to laugh. He lowers his gun, "Zyrian Splatter?! You got to be kidding. Right? If there was a choice given to me, I'd have chosen to be killed and be fed to hungry wolves than work for that unholy scumbag. You don't have anything to be afraid of, Cyrus. Not from us anyway. We only want one thing from you and that is your unwarranted help. We need you to assist us in assassinating that bastard. I guess we can agree on one thing and that your reputation precedes you."

Cyrus finally holsters his gun and Wayne sighs out in relief, "Okay. Now that tensions and paranoia are out of the way...I think it's safe to say that we can try to resolve our troubles together. Right?"

Chapter 8

Steadman who accompanied Colane at Jenny's execution is at The Delphic Fortress. They remove his shoes and strip half of his garments. He is in a long, stone-laid corridor featuring several filthy and primitive holding cells of a cell block. Along with each cell, there are suffering innocent citizens including men, women and children. They are all malnourished and their ribs are showing with hair falling out faster than their teeth. In the last cell in the row, Harris is barely conscious, bloodied, battered and strapped to a medieval torture chair. Big Daddy appears before him, "So what do you need to do to declare the dues that you were responsible for?"

He grabs a voodoo doll of Cyrus standing with a noose around its neck on miniature wooden gallows. He goes ahead and imitates Cyrus's voice in a mocking voice, "I'm an honest man. I can't be blamed for this, your highness and the mighty one, Big Daddy Master Jesse Sparrow...The almighty of all servants! I beg of you, I beg of you, I beg of you, I beg of you to please have mercy on my insignificant pitiful soul!"

He grins maliciously while he manipulates the doll and goes to sit across from Harris in the cell. Big Daddy continues to taunt Harris with this sick little puppet show, "You horrible pig! You committed blasphemy in the name of God! You ought to burn in hell like the hypocritical bastard that you are!"

Big Daddy imitates Cyrus once more as he looks at Harris whose eyes are nearly swollen shut although he is still glowering at him. Suddenly, the gallows floor falls out and the doll gets hanged. Big Daddy cuts loose the doll and holds it swinging from the rope inches from Harris's face while he mockingly taunts, "Oh God! Have mercy on me! Mum! Mum! Help me, Mum! Oh, you stupid moron...Why are you ignoring the fact that your mum...Oh, should I say...Adoptive mum is dead?! She's dead just like how you were dead. It's nice that you cared though. Most people actually give a crap about their real mothers but you're different and that makes you so sweet. Doesn't it? I think I did you both a favour when I took both of your lives on the same day. You two can be together but you decided to come back. Didn't you? Anyway, that was a marvellous performance. I wished it was that easy."

Harris musters up what strength he has and spits in Big Daddy's face. Big Daddy freezes for a moment on the brink of losing his temper but then, he instead, tastes a bit of it with the tip of his tongue and smiles, "I got to admit it was tasty. Do you know what I'd like to call it? The savour of torture. I've never wanted anything from you particularly. I only wanted your scarcely thrashing circulatory to trap that parasitical rogue on the exact spot I need him to be and once you're dead, you'll witness me tormenting your foster son.... yes...I call him your foster son because I know you took him in after his reincarnation and not to mention, you brought him up as your own.

You thought I didn't know that? Well, you are a fool because you'll be witnessing his torment in the final moments of your death. You'll see him with terror before monstrosity. If you're lucky, you might just be able to look at the sinister richness of disfigurement and humiliation that this part-man blood-sucking scrounger will nevertheless suffer.... then the time will come when you will really comprehend how simple you've had it."

Harris weakly answers, "Why don't you do yourself a favour and go screw yourself with the sick little toys you got in your hand because I'm telling you right now.... your time is almost up, pal...?"

Big Daddy laughs hysterically as he wipes the spit from his face, "Come on now. Just stop this saviour crap. Will you? It's a waste of time."

Harris manages to grin at Big Daddy despite the pain, "It won't be long until you actually meet the edge of the knife and trust me when I say this to you.... you haven't got a clue what I have in store for you…."

Big Daddy interrupts himself, "Oh. My bad. I forgot to mention something to you. Receive my sincere apologies because I hate to be the bearer of bad news and I'm sorry to disappoint you, pal but I think you've got it the wrong way. I can't blame you though. These things happen when your head is messed up, especially when you're in a situation like this but just so I let you know it's actually Cyrus who is clueless."

Big Daddy grins with knowing confidence that gives Harris new doubts. He wraps his pointy-nailed fingers around the Cyrus doll and crushes it in his fist as the doll bleeds.

Wayne and Logan stand by Wayne's wonder wagon back in the forest as they suit up for battle. They strap knives to their arms with pistols to their legs and swords to their hips. In the meantime, Cyrus gets set to go as he impatiently drinks from his glass.

He looks around the wagon and realizes that it is cluttered from the floor to the ceiling with sideshow props and bizarre souvenirs from their travels. Cyrus stares at a large show poster, yellowed with age and advertising Wayne's show. It also showed Logan wrestling a monster and Wayne dressed like a magician waving a wand; followed by a young girl juggling a dozen sharp knives. Logan also takes a sip from a glass, "It's alright. You want a drink?"

Cyrus replies, "Yes." Logan pours a drink from the bottle into a glass and gives it to Cyrus, "Here you are. Everyone needs a drink before a mission."

Cyrus takes the glass from him, "Yeah...Hey! Would you mind telling me who the girl is?" Logan continues to drink from the bottle as the drink drips on to his unkempt beard, "Her name is Abby."

Wayne interjects, “Logan rescued Abby from one of Big Daddy's purging innings on a hamlet when she was newly born.”

Logan continues, “I became a rumble when I was in that bastard's military. I was enlisted exactly after the outbreak...I wished I hadn't done it now. I was a lot younger than I am now and not any wiser. I was foolish to think what the difference between good and bad was.”

Cyrus asks with concern, “You never knew the difference between good and bad people and ended up murdering the good ones? I don't understand.”

Logan sighs and takes another huge gulp from the bottle, “Of course, you don't understand and I don't expect you to because it's not exactly alike to how you think. It was never supposed to be like that from the beginning. I was led to believe that we were actually trying to make changes and take charge of stuff for the betterment of the world. But unfortunately, things took a nasty turn when Big Daddy Jesse Sparrow seized dominance and supremacy over this land so much that his military expanded largely. He began to send us to invade cities and attack people's homes.”

Cyrus inquires, “And why would he want to do that? What's the motive behind it?”

Logan reacts, “Big Daddy wanted to grow his empire and he would stop at nothing until he achieved it. I'll be completely honest with you. It got a lot worse than the outbreak. Insanity began to develop more amid his army.... especially when they came to know that they had control over everyone and could do what they wanted.... then everything ended.... what came after was not a pleasant thing anyone could wish for in this world. Everything you see around you is all about homicidal assassination, terrorism, abduction, abuse, molestation, pillaging, sexual assault, maltreatment, mugging, burglary, larceny.... you name it all...."

He gets sickened by the memories as he continues, "It was difficult to imagine what happened back there especially when Big Daddy's army began to throw infants out of their cots and end their lives like they were nothing to them...like they were meaningless...I had finally had enough and chose to discharge myself from the army but it was not as simple as I thought it would be. It came with a heavy price." He proudly declares, "Somehow and some way, I managed to kill lots of those vile bastards. The only thing I failed on is to assassinate the wickedest dregs God has ever made...Zyrian Splatter.

Eventually, I stabbed him but he found a way to survive. Big Daddy never let a soul betray him and get away with it so he went after me and my family. He killed them for revenged. He made sure that it would set an example to the entire nation.... that was ten years ago but it feels like it only happened last night. The only reason why I survived is because I need to.... for Abby's sake. I'm thankful to have her in my life because she is all I have for now. She's the closest thing I got to a family. She is family."

Suddenly, they hear a female voice as Abby appears behind them, "Hey, Daddy. I couldn't help but listen to what you were saying about me."

"You listened. Huh? What did I tell you about keeping your nose out of other people's conversation?"

"I wasn't really but I have ears and I can't help hearing things. I hope it's a pleasant conversation if it's going to be about me." Cyrus turns to see Abby appearing with her attractive face and a waifish physique with dark hair braided into twisting knots hanging from her head. She has a significant strand of hair dyed blue falling down to her cheeks. Her nose has a glimmering round nose ring cutting halfway through the side of her nostril. Her huge eyes in the colour of chestnuts bristling with urgency, she stood on the doorway.

Cyrus senses Abby's fierce aura of independence on her as Logan interrupts his thoughts, "I've been looking for you everywhere. Where were you, Abby? I thought I told you never to wander around at this time in a neighbourhood like this. Why can't you listen for once? You can't keep wandering around, especially when you know there's danger ahead of us."

Abby goes past Cyrus to the other side of the table, "I wasn't that far, Daddy. I was only at the stables. Someone had to feed the horses." She looks at Cyrus,

"Is that him?" Logan nods, "Yeah. Meet the toughest criminal hunting shadow.... Mr. Cyrus Eagleman."

Abby bends slightly and stretches her hand towards Cyrus, "Hi, Mr Eagleman. My name is Abigail. I'll let you call me Abby." Cyrus also bends forward to meet her halfway to shake her hand, "Well it's lovely to meet you, Abby...."

He turns to Logan, "...I hope she's not going with us." Abby slams the table with her fist, "Of course I am. I want to come." Cyrus ignores her outburst and turns to Logan, "I am still uncertain about you and Dr Wayne. Never mind her. She's not coming with us. I am not going to allow some kid on a trip to the evil land. She's not going to be safe there." Suddenly, they hear a strange noise. Cyrus turns slowly to see Wayne pinning himself to his clothes with knives on the opposite wall of the wagon. Wayne looks at them and says, "Okay. I guess everything is well. I'm ready if I have already demonstrated your theory. Perfect."

He mutters sarcastically as he jerks the knives out to free himself, "I guess we have a special highlight for the visitor. It's called, 'You Can't Fool Wayne'." Cyrus turns to Abby in surprise and smiles as she sticks out her tongue. They all step outside the wonder wagon and into the forest while Logan and Abby strap supplies on the Clydesdales. Logan starts with the directions, "We need to go to the primary access road. That will take us to the fortress. After that, we'll need to go southwest from the Edgar Caves."

Cyrus looks worried with a quirked single raised eyebrow of scepticism, "You do realise that this route may very well lead us to a fairly bizarre complex mud war. There has got to be another way around if we want to go in." Logan says, "Trust me. I have spent a lot of time navigating and observing that inferno of a place. This is the only way to go in and once we get there, we will have to access the fortress's swamps without any problems. I need you all to be aware and prepared for this though because what we're about to see is going to put us off for breakfast."

Cyrus frowns with disgust, "What are you talking about? What do they really dispose there?" Wayne replies with a corky tone, "Corpses. What do you think?"

Cyrus turns to Abby's side, "And Abby is going to be comfortable with that I take it?"

Logan replies, "Sure she will. She may be crude and fragile but you haven't seen anything yet. She is a very deadly slayer. That's how I trained her to be." Abby overhears the conversation, "Come on, everyone. Why do you worry about me all the time? Just stop it. Alright? I know how to take care of myself. I'm not a little infant that you used to know, Daddy."

Cyrus holds his hands up in a gesture of defence, "I was only examining the situation. I'll shut up for now." Wayne interjects, "Alright, everyone. Let's check and see if we got everything we need. Once we're in there, there is no going back."

Cyrus pats himself to feel his weapons, "I'm sure we have everything we need, Dr Wayne. However, there is just something that we have missed out on." Wayne asks, "Yeah? And what is that?"

"We need a metal case...." Cyrus answers enthusiastically. He demonstrates with his hands, ".... a massive one."

"And why the hell do we need one for?" Cyrus mounts his horse as he utters, "It's for a particular skull that belongs to an enchantress persecutor."

Big Daddy stands in his garden as he once again transforms and merges at the altar with The Demon King in a bizarre humanoid form and convulses with him. The walls in the garden meld around Big Daddy at the Delphic Fortress joining into his flesh and forming new shapes with his body, "Your Highness, The Ruler of Hell, please allow me to get the agony away from you, for you have endured from countless dead spirits. Allow their grievance to flow into me like a downpour."

Then, burning energy flows from the altar into Big Daddy's body and begins to convulse violently as a strange, power-mad fantasy unfolds in the same grainy style. Evil clowns start to feed on children in the jaws of a mechanical shark along with a demented and insane Santa Claus whipping a deformed Human Reindeer over an orgy of bloody bodies swarming each other like maggots in a river of filth. The Demon King growls, "Bear the endless terror.... of the soul drawing the power of the underworld!" Big Daddy gets excited upon hearing this new fantasy, "This is amazing! Come to Papa!"

Next, he sees bodies bucking and writhing increasingly faster into surreal fragments of jerking limbs and wide, insane eyes; laughing mouths and worming tongues. Big Daddy gets into a near orgasmic state as deformed ghostly spirits of the dead begin to rise from the altar and circle over him before being sucked into his convulsing body. More ghostly spirits emerge and get consumed increasingly faster.

Suddenly, a shrill unholy sound fills the garden and rises to the heavens causing Big Daddy to scream and thrown back. He lays motionless on the fortress grounds. His eyes pop open burning yellow in the sclera and iris while the pupil burns in a fiery red colour making it look like he is possessed. He rises almost vampiric in the smoothness of motion like he's weightless and floats with his arms and raises it to the sky. Big Daddy screams out, "Now the underworld belongs to me!"

Chapter 9

At a wetland, Cyrus, Logan and Abby ride their steeds through a severely overgrown section of swampy forest as a flashy metal case dangles from a short rope off the rear flank of Cyrus's horse. Wayne brings up the rear as damp moss hang from tree branches. They continue to ride in silence except for the soft soothing sound of Abby singing a lullaby. She stops abruptly when she catches a rare sight of Cyrus smiling. Abby looks at Cyrus interestingly, "What's with the smile? Tell me if I'm a terrible singer. I won't be offended." Cyrus chuckles, "A meeting was held quite far from Earth. It was time again for another birth...." She listens and becomes amazed as she joins in to finish the poem with him. Cyrus and Abby jointly sing, ".... Said the Angels to the Lord above... This special child will need much love, Dear Abby."

Abby smiles in wonder at Cyrus and for a brief moment she understands the man a little better as she says, "You're a poet?"

Cyrus glances at her then firmly grips the reins, "I don't know. I'm a lot of things that you can't even imagine, Abby." Cyrus smiles and catches sight of something up ahead and becomes serious once again. He sees a couple of human skeletons re-arranged to form a grotesque bone sculpture up on the crotch of a tree and other trees painted with strange runes and symbols. Cyrus takes them in as he passes by with his eyes stuck on them. He pulls up to Logan and speaks softly, "What is up with all of this witchery stuff?"

Logan knows and doesn't like it either but tries to appear unfazed, ".... I don't know. Mud-chewers maybe or flesh-eaters. Call it whatever you like. You'll find them lynching near the fortress.... they devour the dead bodies they dispose of." Cyrus comments, "They look like primitive man-eating bloodsuckers. Oh God, this doesn't get easier. Does it?"

"Well, the journey to the underworld was never meant to be an easy picking." Logan mutters.

Suddenly, they hear a chilling animal groaning echoing in the near distance. Wayne trots up between Cyrus and Logan, "Maybe we ought to be going a little bit faster. Don't you think?"

Abby starts to sing a song from behind mockingly, "Wayne is a pussy. Wayne is puss...." She gets cut off mid-sentence with a big splash as they all turn to see an empty Clydesdale. Logan shouts after her worryingly, "Abby!"

He jumps down from his horse and swipes through the water. Wayne and Cyrus also jump down to help in the search but Abby breaks through the surface of the water in the clutches of a swamp cannibal further down. She reaches into the water and comes back with a knife and spins before she jams it up under the creature's jaw and stabs it up into its brain. Abby drops its dead body back into the water and turns to them with a proud victory written all over her falling face, "I told you so!" Her facial expression turns into a shocked one, "No way!"

Abby looks behind Cyrus, Wayne and Logan who all turn and sees more primitive man-eating bloodsuckers rising from the water all around them. The horses buck and bolt off as the creatures launch a savage attack but the highly skilled Cyrus, Wayne and Logan snap into action even faster. Cyrus's sword dances through the air as Cyrus seems to fight all sides at once while Logan unloads an endless wall of gunfire into the onrushing creatures and rips them to pieces.

Wayne unleashes a barrage of long, slender spikes from his crossbow as Abby's arms move fast like aeroplane propellers and lets her knives rip into the throats, heads and hearts of the attacking slime. They all manage to kill the creatures within mere moments leaving everyone dripping wet with mud. After the winning battle with the creatures, Logan looks at everyone and mentions, "Is everybody okay...Abby?" Abby replies while panting, "I'm okay, Daddy." Wayne follows to comment, "Yeah. I'm alright. Thanks. I got to admit that caught me off-guard there but ultimately, I find it extremely thrilling."

He turns to Cyrus who shucks off swamp slime and trudges back to his horse. Wayne approaches Cyrus, "Cyrus?"

Logan also tries to call out to Cyrus, "Cyrus?" Cyrus emerges from the dirty slime as he spits out in disgust, "Hey! Chill, man, everyone. Drop the concern. I'm alright. Killing monstrous obstacles is nothing new to me. It just helps to warm you up for the main event."

Logan smiles and slaps Cyrus on the shoulder, "Hey! We may not be the world's greatest team but...." Abby cuts in and says, "Talk about yourself, Daddy. Not us." Logan continues his sentence, ".... we made quite a great impact." Cyrus loosens up and allows himself to grin when he realizes that he's got some good ones backing him up with the fighting. He re-mounts his horse as Wayne, Logan and Abby continue to ride through the muck.

Big Daddy laughs hysterically in his chambers, "....So the entire universe falls and squeals below Satan's luminance. Very soon in a terrific urge, I shall utter a very simple inquest to you...."

He watches the witch-powered and sees a montage of witch trial executions and general mayhem. Big Daddy plays it over while Kimmy dances and mimes to scratchy music from an old record. The rest of Big Daddy's harem of brides arrives to see Big Daddy standing at the centre of a huge feast. Kimmy and Big Daddy's harem of brides surround him and dance on the table while they frolic about the room. The horrible sights on the television seem only to fuel Big Daddy's appetite when he stares at a suspended spread crowd and face down over the table in a hideous device.

He sees Harris and Steadman who are suspended from atop in the same fashion. Big Daddy looks at them and utters, "....and it'll be no different to the bloodless members who are all expecting the spike....to burst the precious, innocent, mummified existence. Now to my very own curiosity, cavaliers, I really hope you both comprehend what an honour this is to feast during my existence."

Harris weakly mumbles beneath his breathe, "Oh God, why don't you just put me out of my misery and finish me off? Go on. Execute me. I don't want another blooming second to be part of your creepy cult." Everyone hears this and the room becomes silence as all eyes turn to Big Daddy. No one dares to speak. Then, Big Daddy begins to laugh and everyone joins in. He abruptly stops and his voice shouts out as loud as a horn reaching every corner of his chambers, "Shut up, Silence, you loony bitches! Don't even attempt to shadow yourselves against my prophecies.... they are my epiphanies of our fresh Delphic universe!" He picks up a large knife and turns to Harris, "Oh you really do love yourself. Don't you?"

".... Then again.... why should I expect anything less from a cold-hearted conceited knucklehead like you especially when you flap your chatty tongue across this place...?"

Harris replies. "You want to talk about flapping chatty tongues. Do you? Okay. We shall...." He playfully places the knife blade against Harris's face and runs it down along his jawline, "Maybe you prefer that I take yours out.... from.... your larynx...." Big Daddy slides the knife down to Harris's throat and presses it harder drawing a bead of blood but Harris does not show fear. He manages to grin once again, "If you want to kill me, why don't you get it over and done with, you psychotic bastard? Go on. Just do it. Do it and shut me up once and for all." Big Daddy starts to get frustrated with Harris as an urge to kill him takes over but a sudden moan from the waking Steadman diverts him. Big Daddy gets distracted and turns towards Steadman, "This is perfect timing. Isn't it? As we can see, our most sincere advocate has awakened. Sir, do you care to add anything with regards to our present situation?"

As Steadman wakes up fully, Big Daddy takes the horrifically seductive Kimmy and the rest of his brides and stand in front of Steadman. They all stare up at Steadman and salivate his greenish-yellow drool. They start to get ready to feast and Steadman realizes that he is the deeply coveted meal. Steadman loses it and screams hysterically while Big Daddy and his brides explode into bone-chilling peals of laughter. They all laugh hard without caring the mind shattering screams from Steadman.

Big Daddy who is still chortling, says, "Interesting performance, Advocate! It's entertaining!" Everyone laughs more as Big Daddy continues, "Right, Girls, I think the moment we've all been waiting for has arrived for our dear advocate to be part of a larger.... communal character in today's celebrations." All traces of mad glee vanish from Big Daddy's face and is replaced by the cold and savage lust of a killer. He rushes forward to slice open Steadman's belly causing a massive downpour of his blood. Big Daddy looks at everyone and takes a spin as he calls out, "Come on, children. Don't wait for me. Get yourselves a drink! Sip from the spark of life down those throats and devour the law-abiding idiot who is brave enough to defy me and my authority." Kimmy and Big Daddy's brides rush forth to bathe in Steadman's blood and lap it up from the table's surface.

The Eagle rides the lazy night air currents in circles over the Fortress as Big Daddy's guards carry Harris out to the garden with his wrists and ankles strapped to a pole.

In the meantime, at the Edgar Caves, Cyrus and Logan walk along together without their horses and lead their way through the filth of the ancient caves. The black sludge waters are waist deep and the thick layers of cobwebs are hanging everywhere. They notice some decaying corpses lining the walls and the stench is overwhelming. Meanwhile, Abby and Wayne walk behind them as Abby remarks, "Jesus! Why does this place stink?" Wayne answers, "Corpses." Abby looks up to the river where Wayne is pointing to several lumpy masses bobbing in the sludge and as they move closer, it is revealed that it's decomposed corpses. Logan interrupts the long stare from everyone, "Right, everyone. We all need to cover ourselves as much as we can. This is not going to be pretty." Everybody covers their noses and mouths with scarfs and bandanas as the first floater slowly moves by. Abby coughs with disgust, "This is too difficult...I'm struggling to take air in...."

"Well just take the air in through your mouth into your lungs, Abby," Wayne tries to encourage her. Abby takes a breath through her mouth, "Oh, God....this is absolutely sickening...." Suddenly, the passageway grows ever-tighter while Abby reaches out to steady herself against a wall thus bringing a row of previously concealed corpses falling on top of her. She screams as the bodies topple over her and knock her below the surface. Wayne hurries over and reaches under the bodies and drags a gagging Abby back to safety, "Hey. Just relax, girl. They're dead. They can't harm you." Logan turns around and calls out, "Are you guys okay over there?"

Abby steels herself again, "I'm alright, Daddy. It's only this dead body that fell on me." Unbeknownst to Wayne and Abby, another dead body rises behind them with glowing red eyes but Cyrus and Logan see it just in time. Cyrus and Logan react and each puts a bullet through the monster's head causing the monster's body to gush slimy ooze onto Wayne and slip back beneath the surface. Cyrus puts his hand on Wayne's shoulder Wayne with a chuckle, "I really apologize about that, Dr Wayne." Wayne wipes himself off, "You don't have to apologize, Cyrus. I knew what was in store for this mission before I decided to tag along with you guys." Cyrus turns to Logan, "I guess we're going to expect more of these ambushes like what we saw. Right?"

"Not really. We should be exactly under the southwest circle of the fortress which is about twenty minutes from here. We can get into the storm sewer once we get there. It's our only way in and once we're in, we'll be able to enter the primary holding cell."

"Also, if I can bet on it, your foster father will likely be there. That's where Big Daddy normally detains his victims before he kills them." Wayne adds. Cyrus shuts his eyes and sees through The Eagle's vision at The Delphic Fortress's Garden. He sees Harris getting strung up like a grotesque figure on a twenty-foot pole. He jumps with fright, "Oh, God. No...."

Logan gets startled and quickly turns to Cyrus, "What's the matter, Cyrus?" Cyrus mumbles with his eyes closed, "Big Daddy has taken Harris into his garden. He's waiting for me. They are all waiting for me." Logan looks confused as he tries to search the dark skies for any clues, "And how did you figure that out?" Cyrus opens his eyes suddenly, "I've just had a vision. I....saw him." Abby catches up with him and inquires, "You had a vision? Did you see him? How? How did you see him? I don't understand."

"Doesn't matter. It's not important. Let's just call it like how I've told you. The ferocious eagle never lies." Abby gestures at Wayne by pointing her index finger to her head, indicating she thinks he's losing it. Wayne smiles because he knows more than what she thinks. Everyone continues to walk further down the caves under a large rusted grate in the ceiling of the tunnel with an endless stream of thick sludge dripping out of it. Logan looks at it and remarks, "I think we're here. Is everyone ready? We're gonna do this. Let's roll." He calls back, "Wayne?"

Wayne replies, "Yep?"

"Do me a favour and pass me a television wire. The one that has four spikes."

Wayne steps up and hands Logan the television wire and Logan swings it up to the grate and catches hold. Suddenly, they hear a distant sound as it hits home and Wayne tugs on the television wire to test its strength. Wayne pulls open the rusty grate, "It's on the mark, everyone." Logan signals everyone to start climbing as fast as they can. Cyrus climbs up the television wire first into the pipe followed by Logan, Abby and Wayne. They all land in a storm sewer. Cyrus inches his way through the tiny crawl space of the storm sewer while the others crawl behind him. Cyrus comes up to a hairpin bend in the pipe as Logan queries, "You guys find anything yet?"

Cyrus peers ahead and responds, "I can see a gloomy beam at about four hundred yards away from here."

Smiley and his two assistants, Wild Jack and Plasmid Bill push a wagon of human remains down the corridor of the cell block and stop at a cage The Delphic Fortress. They begin to unload the grizzly food as Smiley demands, "Get up, Argus. Your food is ready."

For the nonce, deep inside the shadows of the cage, a huge figure moves into the light as the hulking hairy cannibalistic beast, Argus, standing seven-feet tall appears. Wild Jack and Plasmid Bill shovel the human stew into the cell through a small dinner door. Suddenly,

Argus lunges at the door and grabs Wild Jack's arm and pulls him against the cage. Wild Jack screams, "Come on! Somebody! Do something! Come on!" Bill cries out in distress, "Dr Smiley! Help him!" Bill tries to pull him free but Argus gets too strong. Bill continues to scream and turns away for a moment from Jack, "Dr Smiley! Come on. You need to make his blood loss stop!" Smiley holds up his hands and calmly comments, "I'm afraid these are insubstantial tools, Plasmid Bill. I refuse to endanger my job just to save hands down restored servant who happens to be one of my finest creations."

Argus releases Jack who discovers that his arm has been ripped off and blood spurts from the gaping wound at his shoulder. Jack screams and it echoes throughout the corridor. Suddenly, Bill hears gunshots and turns away for a moment. He turns back to Jack and sees him slumping over dead with four bullet holes in his head. Bill gets frightened when he sees blood spurting from his arm and his heart stops pumping. He gets in total shock and turns to see Smiley holding a smoking gun at him. Bill looks at him in terror, "Dr Smiley. What the hell are doing...?! Don't tell me you're crazy!" Smiley thinks about it for a second as he rubs his chin, "I might be actually...I might be...I just can't rule that one out yet." He snaps out of it abruptly, ".... but all the same, I don't intend to have any staff with one armless."

Meanwhile, down the corridor, Cyrus pushes a metal grate up on the floor and spots Smiley and Plasmid Bill further down the corridor as Smiley talks to Bill, "Come on. We got to get moving. It's a bit cold in here. Don't you think? Let's throw Jack's useless corpse to Argus before we go. Shall we? He must be very hungry." Bill shoves Jack through the dinner door for Argus. Cyrus hears the sound of sucking flesh and crunching bones. Smiley and Plasmid Bill walks away, Smiley says to Argus, "Get tuck in, Argus. It's not every day that you get brand new meat. I forgot it's your favourite. It's how you like it. Right?" After Smiley and Plasmid Bill disappear, Cyrus peeks through the grate from the crawl space as Logan, Wayne and Abby wait in anticipation behind him. Logan comes up behind him, "Can you please tell me what is happening up there? What did you see?"

"It seems to me like...." Cyrus stops when he sees Bill and Smiley coming back. He observes Bill and Smiley feeding their chores and says, ".... they are getting dinner ready for the animals." Logan murmurs, "I don't understand." Cyrus looks at Bill and Smiley entering the cell block, "Just wait for a moment. It seems like that crazed doctor is here...Go on...Go on...." Cyrus sees Smiley and Plasmid Bill finally moving off down the corridor, "Right. We're clear. Come on. We got to move." While Bill and Smiley walk past the cell block's hallway, Cyrus climbs out of the crawl space and looks around and signals Logan, Wayne and Abby to come out and follow him. As Logan climbs out, Smiley and Bill are on the corridor but Smiley suddenly stops in his tracks and gets flustered, "Hold on. We need to head back. I just remembered. I need to give Argus his tablets. I'm not going to abandon my latest creation and let it be sick." Smiley and Bill turn and head back down the hall again while Cyrus, Logan and Wayne walk through the corridor of cages looking at the weakened prisoners with pity. As they walk down the hall, Cyrus whispers, "These people. Who are they?"

Wayne replies, "The lost souls." Logan continues to shade some light, "Big Daddy sometimes doesn't kill the people he detains. He makes them suffer instead...." He continues to look at them with remorse as bitterness starts to build up, ".... And the way he does that is stash a horn with plenty of human meat all the time. It's all for the benefit of Dr Louie Smiley of course. He's the one who is in charge of this sick ride." Suddenly, Smiley and Bill appear around the corner and Smiley quickly draws his gun, "Oh. What a pleasant surprise! It's nice of you all to join us." Cyrus, Wayne and Logan move towards him as Smiley declares, "That's enough. Just stay where you are and don't move a muscle." Wayne and Logan stop but Cyrus continues to march towards Smiley and holds out his arms invitingly, "You want to pull the trigger? What are you waiting for? Go on.... shoot me!"

Smiley smiles, "Very well. As you wish." Without hesitation, Smiley fires his gun at Cyrus who takes a bullet to the chest and stops. Cyrus coughs and spits the bullet back out at Smiley. He raises his head and fixates his eyes on Smiley, "I'll probably give you a bull's eye on that so why don't you try it once more?" Smiley repeatedly fires at Cyrus again but Cyrus shows his invincibility. Smiley starts to panic as he fires off the rest of his clip and Cyrus draws his sword. Out of options, Smiley runs behind Plasmid Bill who fumbles with his keys just as Cyrus closes in. He opens the door to

Argus's cage and the giant bursts from his cell into the corridor while Smiley still points his gun at Cyrus.

Smiley fires another bullet at Cyrus, ".... Go on! Try it again and try harder." Smiley continues to shoot repeatedly at Cyrus but he does not barge, "Okay. It looks like you've run out of your leisure time. I'm quite enjoying this game so why don't we swap turns? This time I'll be the hunter and you'll be the hunted." Smiley panics and squeaks, "Hurry up! Come on! Get it open. Go on! Open the cage! Open it quick!" Bill shouts back at him in disbelief, "What? You really are insane. You know he's gonna rip us to death if we go in there!"

Smiley snaps back at him, "Just shut up and do what I order you to do, you idiot!" He orders Argus while pointing at Cyrus, "Assassinate him! Kill him! Execute him! And eat him alive!" Argus charges toward Cyrus with an ear-splitting howl and Cyrus stands ready to meet its charge but in a split of a second Logan steps up beside him, "Hold on. I got this, Cyrus." Logan and Argus charge at each other and Logan takes his sword out and dives at Argus. Logan locks his hands around Argus's neck in a death grip, "Hey, Human-Eater! Come on! Give me your best shot." Argus shifts and gets Logan in an equally unbreakable bear hug. Wayne and Abby come forward to help Logan but Cyrus holds them off for a moment.

As Logan and Argus continue to fight, blood begins to run from Logan's nose because of the pressure build up. Then, with a mighty howl, Logan clenches his fingers with his last bit of strength and they all hear something snap. Argus wavers a beat and his arms fall to his side. Logan lands on the floor and Argus falls with an echoing thud. Smiley and Plasmid Bill cannot believe their eyes. They turn to run but Wayne intercepts them, "Hey, Morons! Where do you both think you're going?" Wayne fires two tranquillizing darts from a small crossbow into Smiley and Bill's backs causing them to fall in their tracks. Wayne looks at them with satisfaction, "Well I guess it's night time for all the bad guys." Wayne and Logan stuff Smiley and Bill in Argus's cell and pile them aside with Argus while they are unconscious. Logan slams the cell door shut behind them.

Chapter 10

Big Daddy sits on his throne inside his chambers deep in his thoughts with his wives surrounding him. Eve enters and humbly approaches as she whispers to Kimmy, "He is not very far. He's a lot nearer to us than you think. Be ready. I think this is gonna be a big fight." Kimmy turns to repeat this whisper to Big Daddy, "Your enemy is here...."

"I already know that," he replies without flinching.

Eve whispers something again, "So now what is the plan?" Kimmy whispers to Big Daddy to pass the message. "We don't plan anything. I'm just waiting for the moment when he will present his whole being to me. I will then show him who will stand tall when he enters within the boundaries of my universe."

Cyrus, Logan, Wayne and Abby move through the maze of dungeons and find themselves in a two-way split in the maze. Cyrus and Wayne shake hands as Wayne says, "Alright, everyone. I think this is where I bid my goodbyes to you all." Cyrus responds, "Yes, all the very best, Dr Wayne. I'll catch up with you on the other side."

"Take care, Cyrus and don't forget that even your low spirits can deceive you because there isn't anything in this God-ridden confine that is not possible." Wayne says to Cyrus. Logan turns to Abby, "Take very good care of yourself, Abby. Remember everything that I taught you. Stay alert...." Abby smiles as Logan continues to talk to her, "Make sure you don't leave Sam's side. Stick with him and as long as you do, you're safe. Sam will keep you safe. He knows what he is doing. Do you understand me?" Abby gets misty eyes, "Yeah. You look after yourself as well, Daddy." Logan gives her a big hug as Cyrus looks and them and feels touched by their affection for one another. While Logan and Abby continue to talk affectionately, Logan assures her, "Once this terrible ordeal is done and dusted, we will move on from all of this and live the rest of our lives happily."

Wayne creeps in and taps Logan on the shoulder, "I hate to break up the family talk but I think time is really not on our side and if we waste any more of it, it will be dangerous. Shall we go?" Logan lets Abby go from the long affectionate hug, "Yeah. Look after her for me, Sam. Make sure she is safe. She's all I have and you know that. She's all the family I got." Wayne bows respectfully to assure him, "Don't worry, Logan. I will make sure that I will guard her with my life." Wayne and Abby head off with Logan watching them with worry and anxiety. Cyrus notices this and places his hand on Logan's shoulder, "For everyone's sakes, I'm feeling confident that they are on the right track." Logan nods and bites his concern back as he turns up to the next corridor, "Yeah. They are. Come on. We got to get this over and done with."

In the hallway outside the Witches' lair, Wayne and Abby creep up the corridor. Wayne gestures for Abby to hang back while he peers around the next corner. A fortress servant appears and dusts a rotten goat's head on a pedestal outside the elaborate door to the witches' lair. Wayne comes up behind the servant and plunges a knife into his neck. He takes his keys and Abby joins him. Wayne looks at Abby, "I guess this is going to get us to where we need to go without any hassle." Abby eyes the door warily, "Maybe."

Abby draws her knives out as her hands tremble a little but Wayne puts his hand on hers to steady her nerves, "Don't forget. We got to get their heads before they stimulate." Abby mumbles, "Chill. I'll take care of it. I'm gonna take them down." Abby nods when she gathers courage while Wayne selects the key from the ring and approaches the door.

The Witches relax inside their lair as some are asleep in their shabby cots while others watch a movie projected on the wall. They look at the other monitor where the autopsy of Colane is being performed in the centre of the room. Wayne slowly opens the door and the door clicks quietly. He slowly turns the doorknob and the door slowly swings open. The Witches are unaware that Wayne has entered because they have their eyes on the autopsy but suddenly, they hear the door creaks loudly.

The Witches all turn with their hockles bristling but find the doorway empty. One of the Witches goes to investigate and just as she gets there, Abby appears and launches her knife at one of the witches. The knife skewers The Witch through the throat. Abby then takes her down and twists the knife to cut the head clean off. Meanwhile, the other witches move in but Wayne gets in their way and wields his sword at them. He swings it at them and slices through one of the witches after the next while Abby backs him up and throws her daggers at them. While Abby and Wayne fight alongside each other, Wayne directs her, "Don't stop throwing the daggers at them, Abby!"

"Don't worry!" Wayne and Abby work as a well-practised team and Abby puts each of them down with a dagger while Wayne goes to slice off the head. They move through the room with great efficiency but they miss one witch who apparently lies dead with a knife through her heart. Suddenly, she rises and gets regenerated as she jumps onto Wayne's back and claws at him wildly. Wayne shouts and screams, "Get this bitch off me!"

Abby appears behind The Witch and cuts her head off with a single swing of her blade. Wayne turns to realize his close call, "I think I got a lot to thank you for, girl." Abby looks beyond him, "I don't think so. Not yet anyway." Wayne turns to see Eve appearing in another doorway across the room. Eve gets frightened and fierce in her outrage when she sees the slaughter of the witches. She screams as though hell itself is being released through her.

Cyrus and Logan both enter the Fortress room from the hallway together and sneak up to two of Big Daddy's royal guards. They grab them from behind and cover their mouths and drag them back into the shadows. Cyrus and Logan appear shortly after dressed like the guards and head towards the stairway. They stop at a heavy wooden door engraved with a demon's skull. Logan looks at Cyrus, "We're here. This is where we need to be. I'm going to see if I can slay as many guards as I can in here but I got to warn you about something. We need to be ready to be killed because I got a feeling that it's not going to be an easy task." Cyrus tries to gather some courage, "Yeah. Tell me something I don't already know. All the best to you though." Cyrus starts to develop impatience and anxiety to get to Harris but Logan grabs him and holds him back. Logan looks directly into Cyrus's eyes, "Before you go, Cyrus, I need to tell you something."

"What?" "Big Daddy's powers have increased exponentially as time goes by. We have to be ready for the worst, Cyrus."

"I know. I'm ready to transport his evil ass to the underworld there and back onto earth if I have to." Logan says, "This is why it troubled me to be precise."

Cyrus gives him the last look. He runs up the stairs with Logan watching him and walk out through the door. Logan enters the guard quarters and approaches the guard station while he is still disguised as a guard. He sees two armed guards standing at the massive double doors. Logan calmly walks up to them, "I really apologize about this, guys. You know I've always been on time but unfortunately, I was stuck in a meeting with Big Daddy." The guard inquires, "You had a meeting? What for? Big Daddy never has meetings with guards.

He'll normally do it with the head guard who is not on duty today." Logan replies, "I understand but you got to understand something else. You got to understand this...."

He unleashes both his fists at their faces and powerfully snaps and breaks their necks. After that, Logan pulls two metal rods out and jimmies the door shut. He takes a small device with a little plastic tube out and slides it in through the keyhole before activating the tiny mechanism causing green gas to start and seep through the tube. The Guards are asleep in their bunks just as the gas seeps in and fills the room.

The Guards stir and cough as they gasp for breath. Logan enters the fortress halls and finishes his business and takes off back down the hall but at the next corner, he meets Splatter. Logan and Splatter stop in their tracks and look at each other face to face as they eye each other hatefully. Splatter calls out, "Hunter Logan. What a lovely surprise?! We don't normally welcome turncoats." Logan scoffs, "Zyrian Splatter. You haven't changed one bit. Have you? I remember how hideous you were back in the days and you still are. I see you looking as ugly as ever. I wonder how your sternum is." Splatter chuckles and responds, "It's doing fine. Thanks. No knives or sword were able to stop me. You know that when you stabbed me, but I guess it's nice to acknowledge a pagan criminal when you came face to face with one. Anyway, I've been hearing stories about you doing well for yourself. You're in the big leagues now. My compliments."

"And there was me thinking that my accomplishments are claimed by your glorious enchantress persecutor." Splatter and Logan continue to fight verbally with Splatter saying, "I'm sure you know all about enchantress persecutors but as far as your old lady goes, the only difference I can make out of her is the fact that she's a....slut persecutor." Splatter draws his sword and steps forward. Upon hearing Splatter insulting his deceased wife, Logan goes into an instant rage, "I think it's fair to say that I've been waiting for this fight for a very long time, Splatter." "Well now that you've got your wish, I hope you've said your goodbyes to your remaining loved ones because you will never see them again." Logan and Splatter charge at each other and clash their swords while they anticipate each other's next blow before deflecting it. As they battle, Logan and Splatter both find that they are evenly matched but kept on fighting.

Cyrus silently moves through the fortress corridors as low-lying fog hovers over the upper floors. He gets around the next corner and catches sight of Kimmy and several other brides of Big Daddy. They beckon to him and then disappear far down the corridor looking like they are floating on the fog. Cyrus follows Kimmy and Big Daddy's wives around the next turn emerging into The Demon King's Garden.

He pursues them through a wonderland of demonic-looking sculptures that continue to form a dark, foreboding tunnel. Cyrus quickly turns as the rest of Big Daddy's wives vanish and take their forms as black cats. The cats rush off into the tunnel of sculptures while

Cyrus continues to walk ahead deeper and deeper into the garden. Cyrus reaches his depths just as the tunnel of sculptures closes in on itself with a whoosh.

Cyrus turns and sees that he is now trapped with no way out. Suddenly, he hears Big Daddy's voice, "Well...Well...Well...What a lovely surprise, Eagleman." Cyrus turns to see Big Daddy standing before him and the cats curled up at his feet. Cyrus does not recognize Big Daddy but he continues to speak to him, "I see that we're in a bit of a predicament here. From a conqueror to a victim, I see that we are standing face to face and toe to toe across each other before our very eyes."

Cyrus asks inquisitively, "Who are you? And how do you know that name?" Big Daddy responds, "Well let's just say that my judgement and philosophy are endless, Eagleman but I'm afraid I can't say the same about you because yours is quite narrow. Isn't it? I mean I can't possibly blame you. Not especially when you do not know what really happened to you."

He leans forwards and smirks, "Well it has been quite a while...."

Cyrus stares at Big Daddy when it starts to dawn on him and Big Daddy continues to speak with great relish in it, "Well first and foremost, in case you don't already know. My name is Big Daddy Jesse Sparrow but you may already know that or hear about my reputation. Anyway, I'd like to offer my hospitality to you as I take you in....to my modern universe of Angels and Devils."

The horrible words echo through Cyrus's mind when he gets bombarded by a series of quick memory flashbacks of the devil killer switching to the gun firing. After remembering that fateful night, Cyrus staggers back a step and gets stunned by this revelation. He stares angrily at Big Daddy, "So it was you?! You're my perpetrator!" Big Daddy grins madly and shouts, "Of course...I'm your murderer, your deity, your God and your conqueror." Cyrus screams out in anger, "Killer!" Big Daddy laughs out loud like a maniac, "Killer! Wow! Is that what you only think of me? Because I'm a lot more than that, Eagleman. It's a shame that you've come to the realization of the unfortunate terrors that you have encountered."

Cyrus draws his sword as he trembles with rage, "My purpose in this world is to assassinate you, you evil bastard!" He lunges forward with his sword but Big Daddy disappears in a wisp as Cyrus hears echoing laughter in his wake. Big Daddy says, "I will take that as a compliment."

Cyrus turns to see Big Daddy standing on the other side of the garden, "Why don't you come closer? I want to introduce you to my new pal." Suddenly, the ground rumbles under Cyrus's feet and a huge black cross erupts before him and rises high into the pitch into the black night sky towering over him. Cyrus stares up at Harris and becomes stunned and mortified when he sees Harris crucified on the pole appearing lifeless.

As Cyrus looks at Harris, he worryingly mumbles, "Harris...?" Big Daddy re-materializes behind Cyrus,

"Come on. Chill for a minute. We're just getting started. He's not dead yet and he can't possibly be.... not especially when we're having this much fun. Trust me, he is still alive. At the moment as you can see, he's only wrecked, out of shape while he agonises across the murkiest lowest point of under surface from my fantasizing powers of invention.... but he does not have that much breath left in him." He grins and continues talking cynically, "It's a shame that he's paying for your sins. Isn't it? I actually feel sorry for him. He's such a pity."

Cyrus turns on Big Daddy with a killer's cold stare, "Let him go. Get him out of here. He's got nothing to do with this. You have me. I'm here. It's me you wanted. Right?" Big Daddy responds, "So let me get this straight. You want me to spare him? Why should I? I heard that he is a bit of a pest. He bears no relevance to this world."

He hisses and continues, "Anyway, I'm sure you already know that you are not in any place to be making demands. In other words, you have no power or influence within the boundary of this fortress."

"I think you'll find that I have.... now free Harris out of this fortress and I'll make good on my word that it would not take me long to take your evil life to the underworld," Cyrus tries to reason with him so that he can free Harris.

Big Daddy gets taken aback and bursts into laughter, "You want to do what with me? Do you want to kill me?

My heart really bleeds for you considering that you have gone crazy just like how you were when you died! You can't do anything to me, Eagleman! Let alone kill me!" Cyrus squares off with his sword, "I will kill you and I will send your soul to the underworld, you evil bastard." Big Daddy continues to mock him, "So you think you can dishonour me? Oh, Eagleman, it's a shame you don't remember...." He leers at him and goes on, ".... that I am the underworld! I don't belong in it!"

Cyrus charges again towards Big Daddy but Big Daddy vanishes again just as Cyrus turns. He searches in frustration when a deep, eerie, all-too-familiar voice rises from the darkness. Cyrus hears the voice of The Demon King, "You belong to me, Eagleman."

Suddenly, the goblins of The Demon King emerge from the depths of the garden as twisted arms snake out to grab Cyrus's arms and legs. Cyrus struggles to fight the tenacious grip but the world around him begins to spin uncontrollably. The garden gives way to another place altogether and also gives way to The Demon King's world and Cyrus now finds himself standing in a weird alien graveyard. Thick fog hugs the ground abruptly and twists around the headstones as Big Daddy appears before him again and gets flanked on either side by winged demons. Big Daddy taunts Cyrus, "You are in The Demon King's kingdom. For your sakes, I wish you all the fun in his world because you're about to live your worthless immortal life endlessly agonising in its clutch."

Wayne and Abby prepare to battle Eve who comes at them and screeches in the witches' lair. Eve looks at them furiously and utters, "You both beauties are now mine!" Abby flings her knife but it passes through Eve and sticks in the wall. Eve cackles as another voice is heard behind them and they turn to see a second image of Eve. The second Eve looks at Wayne and Abby, "You didn't honestly think that you would be able to kill me like you did my parasites. Did you?" Abby and Wayne go back-to-back to counter the attack but suddenly out of nowhere, a third Eve appears and startles them, "Gotcha!" Abby screams while Wayne jerks around. The third Eve says, "What's wrong, Doctor? You are too shocked to speak?" Abby and Wayne witness all three Eves release their unbearable howling. Wayne shouts over the screaming enchantresses, "Try not to be scared! They are only mere hallucinations.... psychological spurs!" The first Eve utters, "Well I have a little present for you that is not a hallucination!" Suddenly, a heavy steel cage comes crashing down from above that traps Wayne and Abby. The second Eve starts to move around them in a circle, "....Oh. You both are going to love being confined in my dark abyss of spirits."

All of a sudden, the floor beneath Wayne and Abby begins to slide open and a pit swarming with zombie creatures screams for them below. Wayne and Abby try to pry the bars open but to no avail. The third Eve rolls her eyes mockingly, "Come on. Make some attempts to get out of this mess. Your demises are far more entertaining this way." "Come on, Wayne. We need to do something," Abby desperately cries out as she tries to pull the bars apart.

"Keep your grip on the bars and say your prayers!" Wayne and Abby cling to the cage bars while the floor opens completely while the three Eves dance around them and cackles with glee. The cage begins to lower into the dark abyss as the zombies' hungry arms try to reach up for Wayne and Abby. Abby throws a panicked look at Wayne but Wayne seems helpless. They draw their swords and slash desperately at the raised hands and arms as the Eves laugh shrilly.

Chapter 11

Splatter and Logan slowly stalk each other at the Fortress halls because both men have suffered cuts and minor slashes from their battle. Logan attacks and lunges at him with his sword but Splatter anticipates his moves and sidesteps him. Splatter gashes his sword onto Logan across the shoulder and incapacitates his right arm. Logan spins around and tosses the sword into his left hand while he continues to fight. While Logan and Splatter continue their fight, their swords clash which causes Logan to drive Splatter back against the wall but Splatter kicks his legs out and sends Logan down. Splatter slashes him across the leg.

Thereafter, Logan drops his sword which goes clattering down the stairs. Logan staggers against the wall as he is not able to stand. Seizing the opportunity, Splatter grins and closes in because he believes he has won this battle and starts to enjoy it. Splatter smiles victoriously and looks at Logan, "Well....well.... well.... well....my turncoat friend. I wonder how your little baby girl is." He raises his sword and declares, "She is so tasty. I think once I've finished pissing on your coffin, I'm gonna give her the pleasure of becoming my latest addition to my long list of sex slaves."

Logan grits his teeth at this as Splatter continues to speak to him, "You know what they say? It's the youth chicks that prevail over the older chicks especially when it comes to producing the finest feeders that one can harvest." Just as Splatter is about to finish him off, Logan notices he is standing under a huge demon-headed sculpture hanging from the ceiling with a rope tied off on the wall.

He draws a knife from his boot and slashes the rope. Splatter looks up to see the sculpture crashing down on him and before he could scream, his sword goes skittering out on impact and clatters against the stone wall, killing him instantly. Logan lets out a sigh of relief as he groans with pain and finally turns to the now-deceased Splatter, "I think it's safe to say that your days of harvesting are away and done with, Splatter." Logan pulls himself up on the wall, limps over to Splatter's crushed body and picks Splatter's sword up. Suddenly, he hears a clamour of feet and clanking armour coming up the stairwell. Logan turns to see an army of Big Daddy's royal guards and mumbles to himself, "God help us all."

Cyrus remains in the grip of The Demon King's soldiers down in the Demon King's World which causing his fury to reach its peak. He cuts free with his sword and slices the soldiers. The tentacles retract again as a howl bellows from everywhere at once. Seeing this, Big Daddy becomes surprised by this and he vanishes again. Cyrus shouts blindly because he cannot spot him, "To hell with your tricks! I've had it! Now let's rise all over this and clash." Big Daddy laughs when he appears behind him, "You honestly thought that these is all fun and games. Don't you?" Cyrus wheels around and sese Big Daddy standing over a gravestone. Big Daddy utters,

"Maybe I can help you out. I've got something for you to think about."

He reaches his hand into the ground and starts to pull something out of the loose soil. Cyrus sees a clump of hair and long strands coming up out of the ground followed by a head, neck and shoulders which causes a harsh recognition to register on Cyrus's face. Cyrus gets shocked suddenly as he whispers in his breathe, "Mum?"

He turns to Big Daddy with anger, "You bastard!" Upon seeing Big Daddy pulling Mrs Eagleman from the ground, Mrs Eagleman opens her eyes and stares lovingly at Cyrus. While Cyrus is still in shock and dumbfounded, Mrs Eagleman starts to mumble with a coarse voice, "Cyrus...." She steps out of the dirt and her form sheds the dirt and rot of the grave. Mrs Eagleman stands before Cyrus looking young and pristine. She warmly and lovingly extends her arms and she puts them around Cyrus and hugs him. Mrs Eagleman says, "Cyrus, my baby. You have no idea how much I've missed you."

Cyrus hugs her back, "I've missed you too, Mum." Mrs Eagleman stares at him for a second and smiles, "Now come on, Cyrus. You have to free yourself from the earth. We don't belong here anymore. We now work for the dead. Not the living. You need to come back to us."

Cyrus gets confused wondering what she is talking about and why she is talking like that. Cyrus holds himself back as Mrs Eagleman continues, "Yes. You need to come back home.... with me and....your daddy. He's waiting for us."

Cyrus gets teary and overwhelmed with grief, "Daddy? Mum...? What the hell is going on...?" Mrs Eagleman smiles lovingly, "Yes, Baby. Your daddy is waiting for you." Cyrus stumbles forward in shock and drags his sword while Mrs Eagleman follows him and cups his face in her hands, "Your daddy and I really miss you, Cyrus. You know we love you a lot even though I did not give birth to you. Come on now. Don't be silly. Just come with me.... come back home with me so we can be a family like we were before." Cyrus looks long into her dead eyes with his emotions running high. Suddenly, Cyrus comes into a realization, "You are not my mum!" Big Daddy realizes Cyrus is not fooled, "That's it! Kill him!" Cyrus gathers his strength and shouts at the top of his lungs, "Go to hell, you Satan's Bitch!"

He rips his sword up and through Mrs Eagleman's body causing her to revert to her true form and die then she turns into a fat, horned Demon. Big Daddy trembles with renewed rage and frustration. As he and Cyrus stare at each other, Cyrus mentiones, "Big Daddy Jesse Sparrow! I'm coming after you next and nobody is gonna stop me. All your games will soon be over. Jokes on you because I'm gonna watch you die screaming. Am I telling the truth?"

Big Daddy frowns with disgust and rage, "What did you just say? Games?! Do you think I need to employ games to overthrow you? I am capable of overpowering you all on my own and conquering you. What?! You don't believe me?! Okay. Just watch this!"

Big Daddy transforms into a moving stone golem, draws a sword in each hand while Cyrus lunges at him and the fight between the two begins. Big Daddy swings his powerful swords with the force of a giant and knocks Cyrus onto his back. He thrusts the swords at him while he's down but Cyrus rolls over out of the way and barely evades the death blows. They trade powerful strikes but neither can defeat the other. While they continue to fight, sparks fly from their swords as they clash. Suddenly, The Demon King swells and growls loudly, "Stop all this! I need you to take his life through my body!" The ground explodes beneath Cyrus's feet and living rock sweeps up from the earth and over his body. His arms and legs freeze within the granite shell and his sword halts mid-swing. Cyrus struggles to break free as the rock solidifies around him with a deep crackling sound. The Demon King declares, "That's it.... now that we are both united, no one can stop us. Now kill him! What are you waiting for?!"

Big Daddy stands over Cyrus as he did thirty years before in reminiscent. He looks at Cyrus evilly and laughs, "Now I'm sure this will bring some memories back. Everyone remembers the final moments of their deaths after their reincarnation so why don't we make the second time worth your while. So, Eagleman, let's do this one more time. Shall we? Just like the good old days, yeah? Welcome to the modern universe of Angels and Devils. I hope you've enjoyed your trip here. It'll be nice if you could stay around a little bit longer. It's a real shame that you have to go back." Upon hearing these words, Cyrus's mind flashes with the haunting childhood images of a laughing Big Daddy who was dressed as the Devil, shooting him and Mrs Eagleman. Cyrus's eyes turn red as tearing drops of blood streak down his cheeks resembling his make-up. Big Daddy brings both swords towards Cyrus's head to crash him as he screams out, "Nooooo!" He breaks free from the stone as a flash of lightning crashes while their swords meet. Big Daddy falls back dazzlingly and Cyrus swings at him. Big Daddy blocks the blow and stumbles from its force. He swings back and crosses swords with Cyrus who dodges the deflection to either side. The swords deflect to the gravestones and split them in two. Cyrus stumbles back against a stone gargoyle which springs to life and grabs him.

Big Daddy charges forward while the swords once again rise to strike but with a superhuman effort, Cyrus breaks free and snaps the gargoyle's arms off. Big Daddy plunges his swords into the gargoyle instead which screams in a spray of blood. He leaves one sword in the gargoyle and turns to face Cyrus. As Big Daddy stares at Cyrus, he screams in a strange, alien tongue before he lunges at him with all of his remaining strength. Cyrus meets him head-on and the force of their collision shatters Big Daddy's sword causing Big Daddy to stumble back. Cyrus realizes Big Daddy has no weapons on him, "I hope you've enjoyed your modern universe."

Cyrus brings his sword down and strikes Big Daddy with all his might causing Big Daddy to explode into a million pieces while Cyrus gets thrown back by the force of it.

Logan, in the fortress halls, gets in the heat of the battle but finds that he is being overwhelmed by the sheer number of royal guards who have him cornered. Logan's sword gets flung from his grip and they are about to finish him but then miraculously, they explode and turn to dust as they dissolve at his feet. Logan stares at the carnage and gets stunned. He realizes something and says, "Crikey! This is unbelievable! He's actually done it!"

Wayne and Abby continue to fight the army of zombies at the zombie's pit and find themselves on the brink of defeat. The zombies climb onto the swinging cage and swarm them relentlessly. One of them grabs onto Abby and drops into the pit with her. Wayne lets go and dives to his apparent death in a last-ditch attempt to save her but then, the zombies burst into flames and fall dead as they quickly turn to dust. Wayne and Abby slump with happy exhaustion as Wayne shouts out, "Cyrus! I knew it! I just knew he'll get the job done. Get in! He's done it. He has destroyed the demon." Suddenly, they hear an unholy scream echoing through the tunnels as the flaming form of Eve stumbles into the pit and lands hard between them. She writhes for a moment and then simply melts. A monstrous ghostly form rises from her body and fades while Abby mutters, "Well I guess we have seen the last enchantress....one dead out of the window."

Wayne and Abby find Logan limping along the wall of the corridor with a trail of blood behind him. Abby runs up to him and embraces him, "Daddy!" Logan grabs her as he lets out a groan, "Abby! You're okay. Thank goodness for that. I didn't think we were going to survive. I guess we got one man to thank for." Logan looks over her shoulder as they hug and exchange happy smiles with Wayne. Abby pulls back, "Yeah. We do. Cyrus! Where is he?"

Cyrus lies unconsciously in the garden with his body covered in blood and ash. Logan and Abby arrive as Logan calls out, "Cyrus! Come on! He's there.... right there...let's go and help him...."

Logan and Abby rush up to Cyrus's side. Cyrus opens his eyes and sees the first sight of Logan and Abby smiling down at him. "He's still alive and conscious. Thank God for that,"

Logan says as he smiles with relief. Abby tries to comfort him, "Yeah. Stay still." Cyrus ignores her and looks around the garden as he struggles to sit up, "Harris....where is he? Where's Harris?"

"Don't worry. He's safe. He's with Wayne." Logan tries to help him sit up

Wayne brings water to Harris inside Big Daddy's chambers, "Here. Get this down your throat...." Wayne does his best to make the dying Harris as comfortable as possible as he holds a cup to his quivering lips. Shortly after, Cyrus and Logan arrive with Logan carrying Cyrus into the room and setting him beside the bed. Cyrus gets stricken when he sees Harris, "Harris...? Are you okay?" Logan signals Wayne and Abby to leave Cyrus and Harris alone as all three of them exit. After Logan, Wayne and Abby are gone, Harris opens his eyes and smiles at the sight of Cyrus he tries to mumbles a few words, "...I knew it...I knew it, Cyrus...I knew that you were going to save me.... it's funny because for once, you did... I thought I wasn't important to you.... now that you've succeeded in your mission...." Cyrus enunciates, "What? Did you really think that I was going to leave you to die? No way. No way in hell, Harris. You're the reason why I survived all these years."

"Hey! I want to let you know that I love you, Cyrus....like you were mine. It doesn't matter to me where you came from. You were all I have after my family were killed. I've left all my will to you.... the house.... the money. Take good care of it." Suddenly, Harris's head slumps to the side and he dies. Cyrus drops his head onto Harris's chest. Unbeknownst to him, the vague shadow of a large eagle rises from Harris and up to the heavens.

The next day, at a graveyard, Cyrus, Logan, Wayne and Abby stand over Harris's grave. Abby kneels before the grave and stabs her sword into the mound of earth in tribute to Harris while Wayne and Logan follow suit. They all sombrely walk away but Cyrus remains behind and stares down at Harris's grave. He kneels and lays down his sword and pays his respect to Harris.

Eagleman

In a Black Forest, The Eagle swoops down and lands on Cyrus's shoulder while Cyrus rides alone through the thick fog with The Eagle flying in his wake.

Cyrus (Narration):

"Nothing comes after life but its demise, the moment it gets into the bottomless scorched. The meeting of cryptic shadowed spirits turned to dust now that the spirits grieve, while the demons wail where my spirit stays in the silhouette, something that remains as a mystery but coming out of the consecrated earth I was lifted, as I am The Eagle."

Cyrus then rides away as he disappears.

THE END

ABOUT THE AUTHOR

Baba Hassan graduated from the University of Sunderland in 2013 with a degree in Media and Drama. *Cyrus, The Ultimate Warrior Underdog* was his debut

novel. Other works he has written was *The Revenge of The Phoenix* and *The Red Hawk* and this new novel is his eighth work.

www.ingramcontent.com/pod-product-compliance
Lightning Source LLC
La Vergne TN
LVHW091102150826
845673LV00002B/689

* 9 7 9 8 8 2 1 2 1 2 9 5 5 *